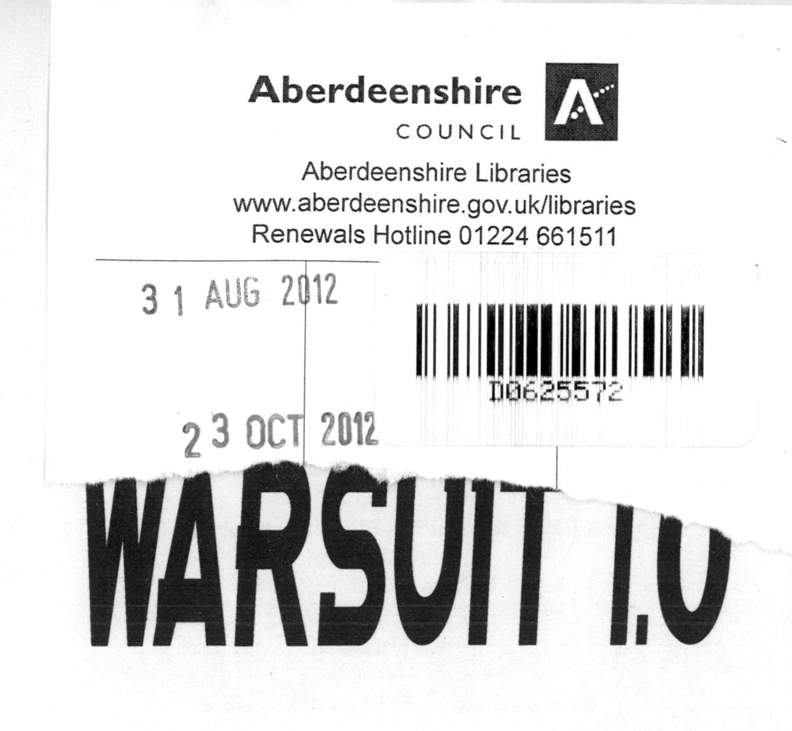

WARSUIT 1.0

QUICKSILVER

AUTHOR'S NOTE

This book is dedicated to Kate Paice, one of the most enthusiastic and inspiring editors I've known.
I owe a huge debt to Beth Marshall and Rob Clark. Both of them made brilliant contributions to the story, fixing my very shaky grasp of physics.

First published 2012
by A & C Black, an imprint of Bloomsbury Publishing plc
50 Bedford Square
London WC1B 3DP

www.acblack.com

ISBN 978-1-4081-5153-2
A CIP catalogue for this book is available from the British Library.

This book is produced using paper that is made from wood grown in managed, sustainable forests. It is natural, renewable and recyclable.The logging and manufacturing processes conform to the environmental regulations of the country of origin.

Printed by CPI Group (UK), Croydon, CR0 4YY

Contents

CHAPTER 1

Od got off the minibus and walked up the track, little knowing that in a few minutes' time his world was to change forever.

He was carrying his school bag and a load of resentment. Both were heavy and hard to bear. At lunchtime Mrs Pilcher had called him to her office, sat him down and given him another of her "you must try harder" lectures. It was the third this term.

"You are one of our brightest pupils, Odysseus Fitch," Mrs Pilcher had said. "You may even be the most gifted boy this school has ever had. At least, judging by your results at your previous school you are. But it hardly shows in your work, beyond the occasional flash of brilliance. Your coursework scores are terrible, and your teachers tell me you don't pay attention in class and can't be bothered to answer when asked a question. You may think it's 'cool' to be lazy."

She did air-quotes with her fingers around the word *cool*.

"But I can assure you," she went on, "failing educationally is no joke. It's your own future you're putting at risk here, and I would be remiss in my duty as head if I allowed you to continue to do so."

She planted her fists on her hips, looking sternly at him through her thin rimless glasses.

"You are on report, Od," she said. "If there isn't an immediate, marked uptick in the standard of your work and of your behaviour, you will be in serious trouble. Do I make myself clear?"

"Yes, Mrs Pilcher."

Her expression softened, just a fraction. "Don't you think it's been long enough, Od? Three years now? It's not that I don't feel sympathy for you, I do, very much so, but… don't you think it's time you started getting on with your life again?"

Od said nothing. The question, like most of the questions his teachers asked, was too dumb to be worth answering.

Mrs Pilcher sighed. "Very well. If that's how you want to play it. You may go."

Od kicked a stone up the track as he walked. Maybe if the stuff he was studying at school interested him, maybe if the work wasn't so ridiculously easy...

No, that wasn't the problem.

What it came down to was that Od just didn't care. There was no point to anything. He was alone. He no longer had a mother. His father was hardly ever home. The two of them lived by themselves in an isolated farmhouse out on the moors, with the nearest village three miles away and the nearest decent-sized town another ten miles beyond that. Od was fed up with school, fed up with his own company, fed up with everything.

Life had become relentlessly, hopelessly, terminally dull.

The track rose to the ridge of a low hill. Od paused at the top. Wind from the moors hit him sideways, buffeting him, tearing at his long black hair, sneaking cold fingers inside the collar of his parka. Ominous dark clouds were amassing overhead, promising rain.

The house waited down in a shallow valley – slate-roofed, grey-walled, bleak. His dad's battered, ancient Land Rover was parked in the open-fronted barn that served as a car port. Lights shone in several windows. This struck Od as strange. The day was gloomy but not that gloomy. It wasn't even four o'clock yet. Too early for lights.

Probably his dad had forgotten to turn them off this morning. That was what you got for having an absent-minded scientist as a father.

Except, "absent-minded" didn't really describe Professor Tremaine Fitch. "Obsessed" did. And "laser-focused". And "impenetrable".

More to the point, the Land Rover. Why was the Land Rover still there?

Od's father was supposed to have gone to work today. Not likely to be back till six at the earliest, although most nights it was normally eight or nine.

Od continued towards the house. The downward slope quickened his pace – that and a gathering sense of unease.

There was nothing wrong, he told himself. There was a reasonable explanation for the lights and the car. There had to be. Maybe his father was sick? But it would have to be some serious illness to keep Tremaine Fitch away from his job.

The moment Od stepped through the front door, he knew the house was empty. You could just tell. The air inside was like a bated breath.

He called out "Dad?" nonetheless.

No reply.

He began to search, room by room. His father's bedroom was in the same state as his own, chaos, the bed unmade, clothes all over the floor. Neither Od nor Tremaine Fitch was a naturally tidy person. Living room, bathroom, his father's study – everything looked much as it had when Od had left eight hours ago.

Except for the kitchen.

On the table lay breakfast. The cafetière sat full to the brim with cold coffee. The toast rack carried four slices of toast, all limp and rubbery. A glass of orange juice looked as if it had not been touched.

Od felt a cold fear grip him then. His stomach flipped. This was not right. Not right at all.

He fished out his phone and speed-dialled his father. The call went to voicemail, with the message, "Sorry, the person you are calling is unavailable."

"Dad, it's me," Od said. "Soon as you get this, ring me back. I'm worried. Where the hell are you? What's happened?"

Raindrops suddenly lashed the windows, sounding like handfuls of gravel being thrown. Od jumped.

He told himself to be calm. Think logically. Piece the evidence together.

When Od left for school at eight, his father had still been fast asleep. That wasn't unusual. He'd been up late the night before, working at his computer well into the small hours.

He would definitely have been out of bed by nine, though. He rarely overslept. He had made himself breakfast, and then . . .?

Then, before he could sit down to eat, something must have interrupted him.

What?

A brainwave, perhaps. Inspiration. Some new breakthrough idea that he had rushed to share with one of his assistants via email or webcam.

No, that couldn't be it. He would still have come back afterwards to polish off his meal. He hated food going to waste and didn't like to go to work on an empty stomach.

Outside, the sky got darker yet. The rain pelted the house more fiercely.

The police. That was the next step. Call the police. Report his father as a missing person.

Od's phone was out, his finger on the "9" button, when all at once the front door whammed open.

Men in black coveralls and balaclavas charged into the house, waving pistols.

"Drop it!" one of them yelled, aiming his gun at Od. "Drop the phone. Now!"

Od let his phone slip to the floor.

"Down. Down on your knees," the man ordered.

Od did as he was told.

The man yanked Od's hands behind his back and fastened his wrists together with a thin strip of plastic. The other men roved through the house, kicking doors open, checking every room.

"Clear!" one of them called out eventually. "Entire site is clear."

"Roger," said the man holding Od at gunpoint. He tapped the radio mike at his throat. "This is Delta Team to Angel Oversight. Delta Team to Angel Oversight. Premises are secured. You're OK to enter."

"Who are you people?" Od asked, voice quivering with panic. "What do you want?"

"Never you mind," the man barked, jabbing his gun into the back of Od's head.

Od got the message. He shut up.

A woman strode into the house. She was dressed in a smart pinstriped trouser suit and carrying an umbrella, which she shook the rainwater off and furled. Her blonde hair was held tightly in place with hairgrips, and her cheekbones looked so sharp you could cut yourself on them. She was beautiful, in a very scary way. Crimson lipstick gave her a mouth the colour of blood.

She stood in front of Od, gazing down.

"Odysseus Fitch," she said. It was partly a question, mostly a statement.

Od nodded.

"Do you know where your father is?"

Od shook his head.

"No idea at all?"

Od felt he was probably permitted to speak now. "Not the faintest," he said.

The woman sighed. "All right." To the man holding Od at gunpoint she said, "Untie him. Let him up." Then, to Od again: "My name is Angelica W-K. I work for the government. You and I, young man, need to have a talk."

CHAPTER 2

"What do you know about your father's work, Odysseus?" Angelica W-K asked.

They were sitting at the kitchen table. The untouched breakfast things lay between them like pieces from some bizarre kind of boardgame. Two of the armed, masked men were standing guard in the doorway. The rest had taken up positions around the house, indoors and out, like sentries. They were, Od guessed, secret service men – killer spies – and they were on edge, gloved fingers nervously stroking triggers.

"I prefer Od," Od said.

"OK – Od."

"And to answer your question: not a lot. Dad's employed at Selston Tor, doing research. It's a nuclear physics installation, yeah? So my guess is he's trying to solve the energy crisis, working on cold fusion maybe, a safe and endlessly renewable power source. Right? Is that it?"

Angelica W-K shrugged, her expression blank. If he didn't know, she certainly wasn't going to tell him.

"Dad never talks about it, anyway," Od went on. "Official Secrets Act or something. And I don't ask. No point, when I know he's not allowed to say anything."

"How has he been acting lately?"

"What do you mean?"

"Have his patterns of behaviour changed? Has he been more furtive than usual? Done anything to make you suspicious?"

"Not so's I've noticed," Od said, thinking. "It's always the same with him. The way it's been for the past three years, ever since we moved here. Work, work, work."

"Anything he's said seemed... well, odd? No pun intended."

Od grimaced. Like nobody *ever* made jokes about his name.

"We don't exactly chat much," he said. "Dad's so wrapped up in himself these days, sometimes I can barely get a sentence out of him. Over dinner it'll be like 'pass the ketchup' and that's it. Why are you asking me all this stuff? What's he done? Where's he gone?"

Angelica W-K seemed to be making up her mind how much she could reveal to Od.

"Your father," she said eventually, "has been engaged on a very important project for the government. A project with far-reaching ramifications. I can't say any more about it than that, although I will tell you that certain hostile bodies – enemies of Britain – would be very keen to get their hands on what your father has created."

"Enemies of…?" said Od, astounded. "As in other countries?"

"Terrorists."

"Oh God," Od breathed. "But – but he's my dad. I mean, he's just a beardy bloke who always forgets to put the cap back on the toothpaste. He's not – not some ace inventor making high-tech gadgets or whatever. He's a boffin, that's all he is. An egghead. A big old nerdy brainiac."

"Your father is, I'm assured by experts in his field, a genius," said Angelica W-K.

"How do you know him anyway?" Od challenged.

"Who *are* you, Miss I Don't Have A Proper Surname?"

"I'm his government liaison," she replied. "The go-between. The one who reports on your father's progress to the powers-that-be, and keep the powers-that-be off his back so that he can get on with his work uninterrupted."

"Oh yeah? Then how come I've never heard of you? Surely he'd have mentioned you to me."

"Why, when he's clearly so good at keeping secrets? Look, Od, what it boils down to is this. We believe Tremaine Fitch has been kidnapped. We believe we know who by and why. What we're not sure of is where his kidnappers are holding him and what they want from us, whether this is a simple ransom case or something more complicated. We have a feeling they're going to get in touch soon and tell us."

"Kidnapped." It seemed absurd to Od, and at the same time horribly plausible. Nothing else would account for his father's absence. "But if he was taken against his will, wouldn't there be signs of a struggle? The house was like a museum when I got in. Like Dad just got up and walked away."

"I can only speculate," said Angelica W-K, "but if they came for him with guns, as there's every chance they did, then he'd surely have co-operated. Maybe, also, they used you as a threat."

"Me? How?"

"Said they'd hurt you, or worse, if he didn't come quietly. Besides, your father isn't the sort of man who'd resist, is he? Not the violent sort at all."

"No, definitely not. The angriest I've ever seen him is when he swears after stubbing his toe, and then it's not even a proper swear word. It's just like 'drat' or 'poo' or something."

"There you are, then. The alternative, of course, is that..." Angelica W-K shook her head. "No, I'm not going to go there."

"What? What's the alternative?"

"That he went willingly," she said. "That his kidnappers made him a better offer and he accepted."

Od pondered on it, but not for long. "No," he said firmly. "No way. That's not Dad. Turn his back on his country? Sell out to the highest bidder? I don't think so."

"Your father isn't quite the pure-hearted do-gooder that you imagine, Od. Nevertheless, I agree. I doubt he'd switch sides. Regrettably, because of who I am, and because of what your father does, I have to consider all the options."

"So what happens now?" said Od forlornly.

"Until his captors contact us, we sit tight and wait."

"That's all?"

Angelica W-K tried to look compassionate. It wasn't a facial expression that came naturally to her.

"Od, I realise how hard this must be for you," she said. "It's a lot to process all at once. You'll have to trust me when I say that we have your father's best interests at heart. We don't want to see him harmed. He's far too valuable to us."

"Why didn't you protect him better then?" Od snapped. "Why haven't you been keeping him under surveillance twenty-four seven? Then maybe a bunch of terrorists wouldn't have been able to march right up to the front door and snatch him."

"Because he asked us not to. For your sake."

"Huh?"

"Your father specifically requested that we would leave him alone at home," Angelica W-K said. "He didn't want somebody watching the house the whole time. He wanted a private life. He wanted you, Od, to be totally unaware of anything out of the ordinary going on. He was shielding you, trying to make life as normal as possible for you. He thought that living in a remote spot like this would be a protection in itself. I tried to tell him it wouldn't be, but your father wouldn't listen. For a brilliant man, he could be pigheaded at times."

"Can be," said Od in a quiet voice.

"I'm sorry?"

"Don't talk about him in the past tense. Dad's alive. He'll be coming back safe and sound. He will. I know it."

Angelica W-K nodded, but a shadow flickering in her eyes suggested she was not so sure.

Chapter 3

Od, up in his bedroom, booted up his laptop.

The secret service men were still patrolling outside. Angelica W-K was downstairs making and taking endless calls on her BlackBerry. Od wanted to get away from it all – the craziness of the situation, the uncertainty of his father's fate, the feeling of dread that was churning in the pit of his stomach. He thought he might lose himself in an MMORPG for a while, or chase down some obscure tracks for his iPod. Something, anything, for a bit of sanity.

He had new email. He clicked to open his inbox.

The first user address that caught his eye belonged to his father. The email had been sent at 12.01PM today.

After his dad had been kidnapped.

With an anxious frown, Od opened it.

There was an embedded video clip which started to play automatically. The face of Tremaine Fitch appeared on the laptop screen.

"Od, son," he said. "If you're viewing this, then things have probably gone a bit pear-shaped for me."

The clip had been recorded in his father's study, using the webcam on his desk. Through the window in the corner of the image Od could see one of the trees at the back of the house. It was in full leaf. The clip therefore must have been recorded this summer, or perhaps the summer before. Either way, months ago.

"This email is on a timed release," his father went on. "At midday every day I must postpone sending it for another twenty-four hours, manually. If I fail to do so, if for some reason I can't, then it goes out to you. Assuming I haven't missed the deadline – and I am a forgetful old dingleberry as you know – then I'm most likely in trouble. Serious trouble."

"You can say that again," Od murmured at the screen.

"So pay attention," Tremaine Fitch said. "This is important. You cannot trust anybody, Od. Least of all a certain rather severely attractive lady who goes by the name of Angelica W-K and is my official handler.

She's allegedly on my side but the only person whose interests she really looks out for is Angelica W-K. She's ambitious, ruthless, possibly psychotic, and I may be a little bit in love with her, which I must say reflects poorly on me."

Eurgh, Od thought. *Too much information, Dad.*

"But be under no illusion – this woman will do anything to get her own way. She will lie, swindle, cover up, cheat, kill. Treat her as you would a dangerous dog. A blonde, sexy, dangerous dog."

That was an image Od was going to have a hard time scrubbing from his brain – Angelica W-K as a Rottweiler with crimson lipstick on.

"Now, here's the rub," his father said. "I need you to do something for me. This is no small favour. If what's happened to me is what I think it is, then there's only one person who can help – the one person in all the world I know I can rely on. You, Od. Angelica W-K will happily hang me out to dry, if that suits her agenda, if that's what her bosses tell her to do. You, on the other hand, are my son, my only child, my only family. I know..."

Tremaine Fitch broke off, looked down, looked up again.

"I know we aren't conventionally close, you and

I. I know life is difficult, especially now without your mother around. I wish things could be different. Be better. I wish we were more like father and son instead of the way we are, just sort of flatmates who happen to be related to each other. Funny – I can talk like this to you now, on a webcam, in a message I hope you'll never receive – and yet we never have this sort of conversation in real life. We're not that type of people, are we? Still, my point is, you're my best and only hope, Od."

"What do you want me to do, Dad?" Od asked, as if the image on the laptop could hear.

"What I want you to do," his father said, "is infiltrate Selston Tor, retrieve my work and use it to rescue me."

"Infiltrate...?"

"You're asking yourself how in blazes are you supposed to get into one the most heavily fortified and well guarded research installations in the western hemisphere? You can't just knock on the front gate and expect to be let in.

"Don't worry, Od. I have it all worked out. I prepared for just this eventuality. Look in my study. Look for your mother. Where she is, you'll find everything you need."

The duration bar at the bottom of the video clip window had almost reached the right-hand side. The message was nearly over.

"Od," said Tremaine Fitch. "I'm asking a lot, I realise. What you'll be doing isn't without risk. In fact, it could be downright dangerous. But I wouldn't be asking if I wasn't desperate. And I know you're up to the job. I know how smart you are, and how brave. Your mother was too. Brave as anything. The way she battled her cancer. She refused to bow down and give in, in spite of the pain, in spite of the side effects of the radiation therapy..." Briefly his face clouded. Then he continued: "You're her son, Od. You're like her in so many ways. So much so it hurts me sometimes to look at you. I know you'll come through for me. I have every faith in you."

The window went blank. A message came up: *Replay?* Od stared at it for a long time.

Did he want to replay the clip?

No. No point. He didn't need to.

He already knew full well what he was going to do, and he didn't have to be asked twice.

Chapter 4

Od padded downstairs to his father's study. He could hear Angelica W-K in the kitchen, barking at someone on the other end of the phone line. He wouldn't have wanted to be the person she was talking to. Whoever it was, she was tearing them several new holes.

He entered the study, careful not to tread on the creaky floorboard just outside the door.

Look for your mother. Where she is, you'll find everything you need.

His father could have been referring to only one thing. On the desk, next to the computer, sat a framed photo of Od's mother. It was a black-and-white portrait that had been taken by a professional photographer almost exactly a year before the cancer killed her. In the picture she looked healthy, happy, beautiful, glad to be alive. She'd had no idea what was lying in wait for her just a few short months in the future. The tumour had been growing in her brain even as she posed for the camera but it hadn't yet got large enough to make its presence felt. This was a photo of a woman who was dying and didn't even realise.

Od swallowed down the grief he inevitably felt whenever he looked at the picture. This was not the time for that, not when his other parent was also in deadly danger.

Where she is, you'll find everything you need.

Od turned the photo frame over. The cardboard backing was held in place by four small fasteners. By twisting them out of their slots you released the backing, with its attached stand.

He levered the backing out of the frame. Beneath, taped to the rear of the photo, was an envelope with his name on it. He unstuck it and fitted the backing into place again.

The envelope felt heavy. There was something hard and rectangular inside, about the size of a credit card. Od ran a finger under the sealed flap and took out a blank plastic pass-card with a swipe strip. The only other thing in the envelope was a small sheet of paper folded in four. It was a section cut out of an Ordnance Survey map of the immediate area. His father had highlighted a landmark on it and written a few words.

Od barely had time to glance at the map before he heard the floorboard outside the door groan. Next instant, the door was thrust open and one of the secret service men stepped in.

"You," he said to Od. "I was wondering where you'd got to. What are you doing here? Thought you were up in your room."

"Yeah, well, I needed something," said Od quickly.

"What?"

"This." Od held up a rewriteable CD he had snatched off the desk a split second before the door opened. "Some tracks I burned for my dad as a birthday present. Some of that classical stuff he loves – Brahms and Bach mostly. I wanted to listen to it. To, you know, remind me of him. Make me feel like he's close and he's going to be all right. Is that a problem?"

The man stared at Od through the eyeholes of his balaclava. He had hard, bright, scrutinising eyes, like a seagull's.

"No," he said. "Suppose not. Just don't go sneaking

around any more. We need to know where you are at all times. Don't want to get yourself shot by mistake, now do you?"

"Oh no," said Od. "Definitely not."

"Because we're on a state of high alert here, as you can imagine. Itchy trigger fingers all round. We hear an unexpected noise, find someone moving around where we don't think someone ought to be, then we're not going to muck about. The lead will start flying, and bad luck whoever's on the receiving end. Got that, sonny?"

"Loud and clear."

"Good. Off you go, then."

Od returned to his room, carrying the CD. The envelope was stuffed in the waistband of his jeans, covered by his long Muse T-shirt.

It had been a close call, and his heart was still pounding. If he hadn't managed to hide the envelope in the nick of time, the secret service man would have demanded to know what was in it, and then it would have been game over. Epic fail.

On the plus side, what the man had said about "itchy trigger fingers" had given Od an idea.

He knew how he was going to get out of the house.

CHAPTER 5

One of Od's bedroom windows overlooked the pitched roof of the barn. On hot sunny days – so rare in this desolate moorland spot – he liked to lie out on the sloping tiles with his earbuds in and the volume cranked up, letting his iPod shuffle through its playlist while he watched the clouds tumble overhead. He was almost happy then, as the sun warmed his body while the likes of My Chemical Romance and Funeral For A Friend lulled him with sweet gloom.

It was now a little after two in the morning. Earlier, around 10pm, Od had told Angelica W-K that he was going to catch some sleep. She'd looked up from her BlackBerry long enough to say that she thought it was a good idea. Her tone had been dismissive, as if she didn't mind what Od did, as long as he did it elsewhere.

He hadn't slept, however. He'd lain fully dressed on top of the duvet in the dark, checking the time at intervals, waiting, listening to the rain rattling down on the roof above him. He reckoned by two o'clock the secret service men outside would be getting cold, tired, bored and bleary. They would be at a low ebb. It would be the ideal moment to sneak out.

He eased open the casement on one of the windows and squeezed himself out onto the roof. He trod along the apex of the roof for a few stealthy, catlike steps. Then he lowered himself until he was flat on the tiles and, inch by inch, he began slithering down.

The hammering downpour of rain was making a racket, plenty of noise to cover his actions, but still he did everything he could to be as silent as possible. The secret service men were positioned all around the house. The nearest of them wasn't much more than fifteen metres from the barn. Od could make out the man's shape, lit from above by the security light on the front porch.

When his feet touched the gutter, Od balled into a crouch, ready to make the drop to the ground. He waited for the nearby secret service man to turn away. Then he launched himself off. He landed with his knees bent, rolling to absorb the impact.

The secret service man swung round. He was sure he'd just heard something – a thump. He scanned the front of the barn, frowning. He went over and shone a Maglite into the darkness within. The torch's powerful beam showed him a beaten-up old Land Rover, a few gardening implements, some rusty carpentry tools, assorted items of household junk.

He shrugged. He must have been mistaken. Ears playing tricks on him. He returned to his post, muttering under his breath about the cold and the weather, and using a couple of unsavoury words to describe the woman he had to take orders from.

Od slipped out from beneath the Land Rover. Thank God the car had a high wheelbase and it hadn't occurred to the secret service man to inspect under it.

Quickly Od searched round the barn and found what he was looking for: a short-handled mallet. It was sturdy enough and the right length for what he had in mind.

He opened the driver's side door of the Land Rover and climbed in. The keys were in the ignition, as always. Who was likely to steal a car out here in the middle of nowhere? Especially a car as battered and crappy as this one. Od's father loved the Land

Rover – loved it with a passion that was all the more surprising given the appalling state of decay it was in – but he knew no one else was going to find it anywhere near as desirable as he did. Hence he didn't bother with even the simplest of security measures.

Od wasn't old enough to drive legally, but he knew the basics. It was hardly rocket science.

Besides, if everything went according to plan, the Land Rover's next journey was going to be a very short one indeed.

* * *

The secret service man by the front door was startled to hear the Land Rover cough into life. He was even more startled as its headlights came on, its engine roared, and the car shot out of the barn at high speed.

He swiftly overcame his shock. Trained reflexes kicked in. Whoever was driving the Land Rover must be a terrorist, one left behind to monitor events at the farmhouse. Somehow they'd missed the guy during the search of the property. Now he was making a desperate getaway bid.

The secret service man raised his Sig Sauer P226 and started shooting before the car had gone even ten metres down the driveway. He emptied the whole clip, all thirteen bullets, into the vehicle. Every one found its mark. Side and rear windows shattered. There was thud after metallic thud as a line of holes appeared in the Land Rover's bodywork.

Yet still the car lurched on, gaining speed.

Other secret service men came running and opened fire too. The Land Rover careered down the driveway and smashed through the five-bar gate which stood before the track that led to the main road. Bullets whanged into the car from all directions. Thc front windscreen vanished in a glittering spray of glass fragments.

Miraculously, the driver seemed not to have been hit. He continued to steer a crazy, swerving course up the track.

Then, abruptly, he appeared to lose control. The Land Rover veered off the track and went bumping and bouncing across the rough, ragged moorland terrain. A dozen secret service men sprinted in hot pursuit, blasting away relentlessly. One of them managed to blow out a rear tyre, and the car began to slew over the thick wet grass. It struck a large boulder with its nearside flank and flipped onto its roof. It lay upturned, still revving, all four wheels still spinning, like some sort of giant green armadillo stuck on its back, struggling to right itself and escape. The secret service men closed in, riddling it with gunfire. They were taking no chances.

Finally their squad leader called for a ceasefire over the comms link. Everything went quiet, apart from the Land Rover's engine, which continued to roar furiously and futilely. The squad leader approached the vehicle with caution, gun held out. He squatted and peered inside.

Empty.

Through the hollowed-out window frames he saw no one in the car. No bodies. Not a trace of blood.

Through their earpieces, the other secret service men heard him swear softly. Then they saw him reach into the Land Rover, switch off the ignition, and yank something out from the space between the driving seat and the pedals.

It was a mallet which had been wedged between the seat and the accelerator. There had been no driver, just the mallet holding the accelerator down.

"A diversion," the squad leader said. "A damn diversion. Everyone, back to the house. Double quick. We've been tricked. Oh, she's going to have our hides for this."

* * *

By the time the secret service men reached the farmhouse, Od was already well away, charging off across the moors as fast as his legs could carry him, heading in the opposite direction from the course the Land Rover had taken.

Rain pounded into his face, numbing his forehead and making his eyes sting. He could barely see in the dark and kept tripping on tussocks of grass and stumbling in depressions in the ground. That was when he wasn't catching his toe on rocks and sprawling face first in the mud.

None of this mattered, though.

All that mattered was getting to Selston Tor.

Getting inside the installation.

Saving his dad.

Chapter 6

By road it was nine miles to Selston Tor, a tortuous winding journey. But in a straight line, cross-country, it was more like six.

For the first two of those miles Od was travelling almost blind. Then the rain eased off, the clouds parted, the moon peeped through, and he got a clearer sense of where he was and which way he was going. Familiar landmarks appeared. The large outcrop of rocks known as Crook-Back Blakey. The two distant hilltops nicknamed the Witch's Dugs. The rushing stream that was either Kelly's Tarn or Kerry's Tarn, depending on who you asked. Od had roamed the moors by daylight often enough that he knew the area pretty well. Orienteering in the dark was tougher, but the moonlight helped.

He wondered how long it would take them at

the farmhouse to realise he had gone. Not long, he thought. The secret service men were probably already combing the moors looking for him, urged on by a furious Angelica W-K. Well, he couldn't worry about that now. All he could do was put as much distance as possible between him and them and hope they didn't figure out where he was aiming for.

By the time Selston Tor loomed into view, Od was pretty certain he had given the secret service men the slip. The research installation, lit up by floodlights, glowed like an airport. It consisted of two main central blocks, both perfectly cubic like a pair of dice, and a sprawl of outbuildings, all encircled by a high chain-link perimeter fence.

Several times Od had studied the installation from a distance and been struck by its concrete drabness, its ordinariness. From the outside it didn't look anything special, this place that commandeered his father's life and swallowed up so much of his time.

Of course, in the light of what he had learnt recently, Od had good reason to think that there was more to Selston Tor than met the eye. A great deal more.

The installation itself wasn't, in fact, his destination. Od re-examined the section of Ordnance

Survey map by the light of his mobile phone display. Just to the west of Selston Tor lay an old, disused slate quarry, a ragged gouge that men had scraped out of the landscape by hand many years ago. Od's father had placed a big bold X on the quarry and added the words THIS WAY IN.

Od was baffled, because he knew there was nothing at the quarry apart from a dilapidated wooden hut that had once served as a site foreman's office. The hut was garlanded with notices saying DANGEROUS STRUCTURE – KEEP OUT, and he'd never given it more than a cursory glance. Was *that* the way in? Did Selston Tor have some secret back entrance?

As he was nearing the quarry, Od's phone vibrated in his pocket. He took it out. He had a new text message.

From his father!

He opened it excitedly, feeling relief and hope flutter like a bird's wings in his belly. Maybe Dad was OK. Maybe he'd outwitted his terrorist captors and escaped and he was texting Od to share the good news. Maybe this whole nightmare was over.

The text read:

Apologies, Od, this is just another timed-release message. I've configured it so that it'll be activated the moment your phone's GPS puts you within a 500 metre radius of the quarry.

I'm assuming you've already got the map and pass-card. Otherwise why would you be where you are now? OK, so you know that old hut in the quarry. That's what you should be concentrating on.

Don't just go blundering straight inside, though. It's not what it appears, not simply an abandoned tumbledown shack. For one thing, it's guarded. There's an armed soldier. He goes out on patrol regularly, on the hour every hour. His sweep of the quarry takes him four minutes, so that's how long you have to get inside without being spotted. The rest should be self-evident.

```
If you need a hint, just remember the
proudest day of my life and the first
day of yours.

Best of luck. I have every faith in
you.

Dad
```

Od checked the time. It was ten to four. Ten minutes till the soldier made his rounds. He'd better hurry.

* * *

Od arrived at the quarry's edge cold, bedraggled, damp, footsore, exhausted, but pumped with adrenaline. He found a hiding place with a clear line of sight to the hut, which butted up against a sheer cliff-face, a rugged dark curtain of stone. Now that the rainclouds had cleared the moon shone down, gibbous and bright, illuminating the scene. The radiance from the floodlights at Selston Tor helped, too. Od could see everything almost as well as if it was daytime.

Not a chink of light glimmered through the boards that were nailed over the hut's windows. Could there really be a soldier in there?

3:59. In a minute's time, he would know.

Sure enough, at 4am precisely, the hut door rattled open and out came a man. He wasn't dressed like a soldier. Didn't look like one in the least. If anything, he looked like a tramp, a homeless person who'd taken shelter in the hut for the night. His clothing was ragged and ill-fitting. Plastic carrier bags were wrapped around his shoes as makeshift waterproofing. He wore a grotty old baseball cap on his head, and both his jeans and his jacket were full of holes. He paused to allow his eyesight to adjust to the darkness, then started to walk away from the hut, and away also from where Od was hiding. He moved as a tramp might, bent over, dragging his feet.

And yet...

The way he kept looking around him did not seem tramp-like. His head turned left and right with rapid, alert movements as he shuffled across the quarry. He seemed wary, vigilant for anything out of the ordinary.

That and the fact that he had emerged from the hut exactly on the hour, just as the text from Od's dad had predicted, told Od that he should not be fooled. The tramp *was* a soldier. And under those tatty, threadbare clothes there surely had to be a gun in a holster. The message had said "armed", hadn't it?

The tramp-soldier had gone perhaps a couple of hundred metres from the hut. Od stirred himself to get going. It was now or never. He broke from cover and darted towards the hut. He ran on tiptoes, avoiding heaps of loose broken slate and sticking to firm ground. He reached the door and dived through. There was a second, much newer door just inside, and he dived through that too.

The hut turned out, like the soldier's clothing, to be a disguise, a false front. It was a shabby timber shell that had been erected around a windowless prefab unit. Inside, the prefab was bright and blissfully warm thanks to an electric space heater. Od saw a canvas chair, a stack of magazines, a Nintendo DS, a lunchbox and a thermos flask, which showed how the soldier occupied his time between patrols. There was also a circular steel door filling almost all of the wall on the side of the prefab that lay adjacent to the cliff-face.

Od went straight to the door, which reminded him of the entrance to a bank vault – it was that massive and sturdy. It lacked any kind of handle but an electronic keypad lock was mounted at its centre. Od fished out the pass-card and swiped it through the slot. On a tiny screen above the keypad, a message appeared:

PLEASE ENTER YOUR CODE, PROFESSOR FITCH

Below were eight empty boxes. An eight-digit number had to be inputted.

Just remember the proudest day of my life and the first day of yours, the text had said. His father clearly meant the day his only child was born. Od was strangely touched by the choice of wording.

He tapped in the date in numerals – day, month, year. Something clunked deep within the door. Then something clanked. Then the door swung ponderously inward.

Ahead lay a broad, dimly lit tunnel that seemed to go on forever, hollowing into the hillside.

Od entered. After a few steps, he hesitated. He had no idea what lay ahead. The tunnel reeked of damp, dirt, and the dusty residue of eons of geological time. Its rock walls were like the gullet of some vast mythical beast that could swallow a teenager whole without even noticing. He was – he couldn't deny it – scared.

Then the door thudded shut behind him, with firm finality.

That was that. He was committed. No going back now.

Chapter 7

The tunnel wasn't a secret back entrance. It was an emergency exit. Signs posted at intervals along its length bore red arrows pointing urgently back the way Od had come. The signs also advised people to stay calm and not run. Should something go wrong at the installation, workers were supposed to use this tunnel to get out, and do so in an orderly fashion.

Od supposed it was best not to panic if disaster struck at a nuclear research installation. Still, he didn't think *he* would be able to keep a clear head under such circumstances. He'd be scrambling over everyone else and elbowing slowcoaches aside to reach safety.

That was assuming what they did at Selston Tor was nuclear-based stuff. Od wasn't convinced about that any more, or about anything. What if it was worse than nuclear? Biological, for instance. Something with military applications. Genetically engineered killer viruses, maybe. New and ever more horrible ways of wiping out your enemies.

Oh Dad, what have you been up to? What the hell have you got yourself involved with?

The tunnel terminated eventually at a door similar to the first, with an identical electronic lock. Od guessed he must have reached the installation itself. He was directly below the surface buildings, deep underground.

On the other side lay the truth. Once through this door, Od would discover what had been keeping his father so busy these past three years and why they'd moved to this godforsaken part of the country and why they'd been living a life of such suffocating separateness and solitude. The *real* reason for all those things.

Od hesitated. He almost didn't want to know the answers.

But then, he had no choice.

* * *

The echoes of the door closing boomed hollowly through a cavernous space, soon getting lost somewhere up among the steel crossbeams in the ceiling. A handful of low-wattage red lights silhouetted banks of machinery, computer consoles, workbenches, lathes, cutting gear, welding equipment. Od felt as if he had walked into an industrial plant, a high-tech factory for constructing large and elaborate metal artefacts. Or perhaps a sculptor's studio.

Confirming this impression was the fact that everything in this chamber was focused around a central platform and what stood on that platform.

It was a bizarre kind of statue, at least seven metres from top to toe, a chunky, robot-like representation of a human being. Od moved closer to it, both puzzling and marvelling at once.

The statue had a squat head the size of a space hopper, inset with glassy black eyes like two snooker balls. Arms protruded from beneath bulky, out-jutting shoulders, each as broad in diameter as a beer keg and as long as Od himself was tall. A tapered waist led to powerful-looking legs that seemed to be sheathed in knee-length buccaneer boots. The one human attribute the statue lacked was hands. Its right arm ended in a profusion of different-sized tubes, like pipes ranging from pea shooter to rain gutter. Its left arm sported what appeared to be a cross between a satellite dish and a set of pincers.

In all, with its beetling brow and weightlifter's build, the thing gave off an air of might and menace. The lighting lent a blood-red tinge to its shiny orange and black striped surfaces. There were slots and flaps all over its torso and recessed vents in its legs. Cables of varying thickness were attached to it in different places, like a host of umbilical cords. The statue – if that was what it was – seemed to be waiting for something. To be born, maybe.

Yes, thought Od. That was what was so uncanny about it. It was an automaton that looked ready to move, to act, to function, completely independently. All it needed was some kind of spark to set it going, a bit like the patchwork monster in those old horror films that was nothing but dead body parts sewn together until Dr Frankenstein called down the lightning and gave it life.

Tremaine Fitch was a software expert primarily, although he had a degree in engineering too. This was what had preoccupied him for three years? This was what he had been devoting himself to? This was why terrorists had taken him hostage?

Od hopped up onto the platform and walked warily in a circle round the robot statue. At the rear he found a small stepladder which led up to an open hatchway in the back of the thing. He couldn't resist the temptation to climb up and take a peek inside.

The moment he did so, everything made sense. In the interior of the statue there was a person-shaped space, a metal support cradle with just a small amount of padding for comfort. Facing this was an array of screens, interspersed with readouts and displays, like a control panel, an elaborate dashboard.

Not a statue.

Not a robot.

A vehicle. Something you piloted.

A walking, four-limbed tank.

A war machine.

So no wonder his dad had been kidnapped. No wonder government military officials were in such a flap about it all.

Tremaine Fitch had been helping to build an extraordinary new form of battlefield weapon.

Od was stunned by the revelation. He'd always thought of his father as a peace-loving guy. Liberal in outlook. The sort who avoided conflict and abhorred violence. A live-and-let-live type.

How wrong could you be?

He felt dizzy, a little sick. He had to place a hand on the war machine's cold metal skin in order to support himself and not fall off the stepladder.

As he did so, it seemed he jarred something. The machine's interior lit up all of a sudden, as if roused from slumber. The screens flickered into life. A deep, heavy hum began, filling the war machine's frame.

From within came a voice, buzzy and artificial. "Presence detected. Identify," it demanded.

Od gaped.

"Repeat: identify," the machine said.

"Uh..."

"Voice recognition running. Identity confirmed as Odysseus Fitch."

"What?"

"Hello, Od." The voice abruptly altered. Its tone was more youthful now, and less abrasive.

"Me? You know who I am?"

"Of course I know who you are," the machine said. "And surely you recognise me?"

"Er, no. I mean, this is the first time I ever set eyes on you. Five minutes ago I didn't even know you existed."

"But my voice. Familiar, isn't it?"

It was. Od just couldn't work out why.

Then he got it.

"That's... that's *my* voice," he said.

"Bingo. Synthesised by your father, an exact simulation of your pitch, register, timbre and speech patterns."

"Not that exact. 'Bingo'?"

"He tried his best," said the machine. "The point of it is to provide reassurance and establish an instant rapport between the two of us."

"Look," said Od. "What's going on? This is all a little bit nuts. I'm talking to a, what, a computer program – some kind of artificial intelligence software that's talking back to me in my own voice. I shouldn't even be here. I'm just following my dad's instructions."

"Yes, Professor Fitch had a feeling there was a chance you and I might meet one day. I just wish it was under better circumstances. I can only assume something bad has happened to him."

"If by bad you mean pigging disastrous, then yes, it has."

"Then your next step should be to climb into me."

"Huh? Come again?" Od scowled at the machine.

"Climb into me. Your father needs me. Needs *us*."

"Us? In what way?"

"To retrieve him from wherever he's being held prisoner."

"You..." Od began, now nothing short of flabbergasted. "You mean me in you? You with me? Together?"

"That's the general meaning of the term 'us', Od. Both you and I, working in tandem, can get the professor out of the fix he's in."

"You want me to get into you and – "

"Is the concept really so difficult to grasp?" said the machine, with something close to a sigh. "I need a pilot. Your father needs a rescuer. You are the man for both jobs."

"But I can't even drive a car," Od protested. "How am I supposed to be able to work a complicated piece of kit like you?"

"Don't be so modest. You're super-smart, while I'm actually surprisingly straightforward to operate. My control interface, designed by your father, is very user-friendly. You can walk, right?"

Od nodded.

"If you can do that, you're halfway there with me. So get in."

"No, I..."

"I don't think we have time to debate this. Do you want to help your father or not?"

"Dumb question."

"Then get in. The sooner we start to bond, the sooner we can – "

The machine broke off.

"What?" said Od. "The sooner we can what? And what do you mean by bond?"

"Uh-oh," said the machine.

"'Uh-oh'?" echoed Od.

"Trouble. Upstairs. I'm registering automatic rifle fire. Multiple sources, multiple locations."

"I don't hear anything."

"Forgive me, but you don't have the sensory resources I do. It appears to be some kind of incursion. Numerous hostiles. Their forces are attacking the installation's defenders. And, I'm afraid, overwhelming them."

Faintly now, Od could hear a sporadic crackling noise. It originated from overhead, far away, muted by thick walls and floors. But it did sound, to the best of his knowledge, like exchanges of gunfire.

Then an alarm began to whoop, resounding through the chamber like the braying of a frightened donkey.

"You have no choice, Od," the machine said. "They're heading this way, and I'm the safest place you can be, believe me. Perhaps the only safe place."

"But aren't these – these *hostiles* coming for you?"

"A sensible deduction. More than likely they are. But that doesn't change the truth of what I said. If anything, it reinforces it. Hurry. Move. Now."

Od didn't see that he had an alternative. He bent his head and clambered in through the hatch. He lowered his legs into the two cylindrical cavities provided.

Almost immediately, the hatch sealed shut behind him. A set of sliding plates hissed together like the shutter of an old-fashioned camera.

"Welcome aboard," said the machine. "Before we go any further, I should introduce myself properly. My official designation is Warsuit One Point Oh. But you can call me Wes."

CHAPTER 8

"Wes?" said Od.

"It stands for Weaponised Exoskeleton System. Wes is less of a mouthful."

"Fair enough, Wes. I'll call you that if you'll do one thing for me."

"Of course. What is it?"

"Can you somehow change your voice? It's creepy being spoken to by myself."

"No problem. I'll go back to my default setting." The voice became the synthetic, impersonal one Wes had first used. "How is that?"

"You have anything else?"

"I have a library of over four hundred voice simulations to choose from. Reconfiguring. How about this? An improvement?"

Wes sounded human again but now his voice was

that of a small girl, a lisping primary-schooler who spoke at piccolo pitch.

"Yeah, that's also creepy. Sounds like you should be playing with Bratz dolls or Sylvanian Families or something."

"What would you prefer?" Still the little girl, Wes spoke with a touch of petulance. "The prime minister? The president of the United States? Angelica W-K?"

"No, no, and definitely no. Dad programmed you with *her* voice? He's been single far too long. Tell you what, can you do his?"

"Your father's voice? Accessing Tremaine Fitch file. All right? This more like it?"

It was eerie, hearing a perfect replica of his father's voice coming out of Wes. But it felt somehow right, too. Fitting.

"It'll do," said Od.

"Well, now that we've got that sorted, let me show you what we're up against," said Wes. "I'm patching myself wirelessly into the Selston Tor security camera feeds."

Crisp CCTV images popped up on three of the screens in front of Od. They showed people clad in grey one-piece battle fatigues, running through corridors, firing strange stubby machine guns.

Soldiers were shooting back with assault rifles, but it was clear there were far fewer people defending the installation than there were attacking. Not only that but the intruders' guns seemed superior. Heavily outnumbered, the soldiers were going down.

"Who *are* they?" Od said, horrified.

"Their garb is distinctive," replied Wes. "The squarish helmet, the mask with inverted-triangle faceplate, the grey jumpsuit with chunky polyethylene-fibre panels – it's the signature uniform of the paramilitary arm of the global terrorist network known as T-Cell."

"T-Cell? Never heard of them."

"Nor should you have. Every legitimate government in the world has done its utmost to deny and suppress all evidence of their existence. They're dangerous fanatics with a mania for high-tech inventions."

"Like those guns of theirs, for instance? The ones that look a bit like dust busters?"

"Yes. Wave cannons, they're called. The Ministry of Defence is working on its own prototype for use by the British army. Instead of a single stream of bullets one after another, the wave cannon fires a dozen simultaneously in a horizontal S-shaped burst.

Hard to miss with that."

"So what's their angle, this T-Cell lot? Their political ideology? What do they want?"

"Plenty of things. But right now: me. They're coming down here, to this very chamber."

On one of the screens, two of the T-Cell operatives were outside a large steel door, setting up some sort of projector device on a tripod.

"That there is the ground-level access to the lifts," said Wes. "The entire installation has gone into automatic lockdown, and all the inner doors have sealed themselves. They're bombproof, virtually impregnable. T-Cell, however, don't seem to think that's a problem."

As Od watched, the T-Cell operatives set the device going, standing well back from its funnel-shaped nozzle. There was a piercing whine and the door began to judder and blur, and then, incredibly, to crumble. Fragments of it flaked off, falling to the floor in a heap, as though the door was rusting away at super high speed, decades of decay taking place in seconds. Soon there was a large, almost perfectly round hole.

"A drill that uses focused ultrasonics. Not much can resist that."

"You seem impressed," said Od.

"I admire the appliance of technology. The downside is it means they'll be swarming all over us in, I estimate, less than three minutes."

"Then we have to get out of here."

"Agreed."

"Well... what are you waiting for?"

"The command."

"From who?"

"From *whom*, Od," Wes corrected.

"Sorry, Dad – I mean, Wes."

"You're the pilot," Wes said. "I'm just a craft. I can't go anywhere without your say-so."

"Right. So, to walk, I just move my legs, yeah?"

"Yes, but don't you think we should release the diagnostic and charge cables first? Otherwise we'll be dragging along half the lab equipment with us."

"That's probably a good idea."

"Give the order, then."

"Um, release the cables, Wes."

The main screen was labelled "External View [Head]". On it, Od saw the cables drop away from Warsuit 1.0 and slump to the floor like so many stunned snakes.

"Now," said Wes, "you may want to insert your

arms into the apparatus to your right and left. Walking's easier if you counterbalance the movement of your legs by swinging your arms."

"Like this?" Od slid his arms into a pair of jointed slings on either side.

"Like that. And off we go. Best foot forward."

Od shifted his right leg gingerly. Warsuit 1.0 responded with surprising suddenness, shuffling its right foot across the platform.

"Wow, I thought that would be more of an effort."

"You're thinking of me as though I'm some sort of high-tech medieval suit of armour," said Wes. "I'm not. I have stabilising gyroscopes and muscle-amplifying servomotors. I'm built to enhance your natural movements, not hinder them. Try the other leg. Take a proper step this time."

Od did. Warsuit 1.0 wobbled a little but stayed upright.

"Major-league weird," he said.

"I know, but you'll get the hang. Just bear in mind that I'm considerably bigger than you and therefore have a much longer stride. You'll need to adjust your spatial aware–"

Od, who had been concentrating on taking the next step, suddenly found the suit tipping forwards. Next thing he knew, there was an almighty *CLANG!!!* and he was horizontal and had bashed his mouth on one of the screens.

"Ow!"

"As I was saying," said Wes, "you'll need to adjust your spatial awareness accordingly. We fell off the edge of the platform and now we're lying prone on the floor."

"Well, how do we get up? We're not stuck, are we?"

"It would be pretty daft if we were."

"Do I shove off with your arms to get us upright?"

"I wouldn't. The Warsuit doesn't have hands. It has weapons. Shoving off with them may damage them."

"Oh. So what do we do?"

"Might I recommend deploying the forward thrusters?"

"You have forward thrusters?"

"I have omnidirectional thrusters. How else would I be able to fly?"

"You can fly!?"

"Yes, but one thing at a time. Let's not run before we can walk, as it were. By the way, the T-Cell operatives have reached the lifts and are coming down. We really should get a wiggle on."

"Then fire up those thrusters."

There was vibration, rumbling, shuddering. Od felt the Warsuit lifting up through ninety degrees, rising to vertical.

"There," said Wes as the vibration faded. "You cried out a moment ago. Are you OK?"

"Bashed my lip. I'll live. Which way now?"

"Your call."

"But you know the layout of this place."

"Well, you came in via the emergency exit, didn't you? I suggest we leave the same way. The tunnel has just enough clearance for me, if I duck."

Od stomped towards the vault-like door. The Warsuit's progress, with its novice pilot at the helm, was far from graceful. It collided with a workbench, shunting it aside as though it weighed just a few kilogrammes rather than several hundred. It also accidentally struck one of the computer consoles with its thigh. The blow was glancing but nonetheless smashed the console to smithereens.

"Aargh," said Od. "Not good."

"You're doing fine," Wes said encouragingly. "I reckon I'm doing pretty well too, seeing as this is my maiden voyage. Every bit of me is in good working order, so far. Fully responsive. All systems nominal."

"Maiden voyage? This is the first time you've walked?" Od found it hard to believe.

"First time I've set foot off that platform. Oh, there've been *in situ* tests. Plenty of them. Lifting a leg, waving an arm. But that's about as far as it goes. I've not actually *been* anywhere, till today. You're officially my first proper pilot."

"I'm honoured."

"You should be. Door's straight ahead."

"I know." Od halted. "I've just had a thought. I'll need to get out of the suit to use the pass-card."

"Or," said Wes, "you could simply blow the door out of its frame."

"Yeah, ha ha, right, there's always that."

"I'm serious. Do you have any idea the level of firepower I'm packing?"

"Obviously I don't."

"Perhaps you should find out. That door is fifty-six point five centimetres thick, give or take a millimetre, and made of steel-clad concrete. Would you like me to configure my right arm to launch a blockbuster shell?"

"Yeah, sure, why not?" To Od it seemed absurd; hilarious. Fire a whacking great shell at the door? Of course! What could be more normal?

The barrels at the end of Warsuit 1.0's right arm spun until the largest of them locked into position.

"Raise your right arm, Od. I can do the rest."

Od brought his arm up, levelling it at the door.

"Targeting," said Wes.

Crosshairs on the main screen sighted on the hinge side of the door, its weak spot.

"Awaiting launch command."

"OK. Bombs away."

"You'll want to brace yourself. We're close to the impact point. There will be some blowback from the blast, in addition to the firing recoil."

The blockbuster shot from the Warsuit's arm. A split second later a tremendous, *whoomph*ing explosion pummelled the door backwards out of its frame as though it were made of nothing more than hollow tinfoil. The door sailed down the tunnel, bouncing off the walls and coming to rest flat on the floor some thirty metres away.

Inside the Warsuit, Od was rocked and buffeted.

He was also, in another sense, staggered.

"Whoa," he said. "Did I really just do that?"

"You really just did. And those T-Cellers are really just outside and about to break in any second."

Sure enough, with a shrieking whine the door at

the opposite end of the chamber began to disintegrate. Od saw it on the screen labelled "Rear View". As soon as a sufficiently large gap had appeared, in ran a dozen T-Cell operatives, assault rifles at the ready.

"You have a choice," Wes said. "We can either stand our ground and fight, or take evasive action."

"By fight, you mean kill."

"T-Cell want the Warsuit. They'll do anything to get their hands on it. We have to be prepared to do anything to prevent them succeeding."

Od thought fast. He was no killer. He'd never even thrown a punch in anger. "Dad's the priority. The sooner I get to him, the better."

"Fine. Evasive action it is. Let's go."

Od bent forward and headed into the tunnel.

CHAPTER 9

Bullets blizzarded around Warsuit 1.0 as it pounded along the tunnel, hunched over. Wes reassured Od that the suit's armour plating could easily withstand conventional gunfire. Still Od flinched as he heard the rippling whine of rounds ricocheting off metal.

"Why are they even shooting at us?" he yelled as he ran. "Surely they want the suit intact."

"I'm eavesdropping on their comms chatter," said Wes, "and from what I'm hearing, they weren't expecting anyone to be in the suit. They reckon you're a civilian, one of the boffins who built me, and they think they can intimidate you into surrendering. There's fear in their voices, too. I think the penalty for failing in their mission will be quite severe."

"Remind me to feel sorry for them later. Hey, we're losing them."

"We are. I may galumph somewhat, but when I get going, I can shift."

"How much further to the end of the tunnel?"

"Four hundred and forty metres. Four hundred and thirty. Four hundred and – "

"OK, now listen," said Od, panting a little from the exertion of running. "We can't just hit the next door with a shell like we did the last one. There's a soldier posted right the other side."

"I predict he wouldn't survive the blast."

"I predict that too. What other options do we have?"

"Several," said Wes. "A super-focused beam of microwave radiation. A magnetised nano-thermite charge. A squirt of carborane superacid. Any of those would do the trick."

"You have all that on board?"

"And more. I'm extraordinarily well equipped. Fitted for every conceivable combat scenario, be it battlefield or black ops."

"The microwave thingy sounds a bit iffy as far as that guy outside's concerned, though. And the magnetised charge."

"True. And the acid, highly corrosive as it is, might take too long eating through all that steel and concrete. We don't want to be a sitting duck.

The T-Cellers could get it in their heads to use their ultrasonic drill on us. I suppose I could simply hack into the lock and open the door that way."

"That's more like it," said Od. "Wait." He frowned. "If you can do that, why didn't you suggest it when we were opening the first door?"

Wes hummed a tuneless tune to himself. It was something Od's father sometimes did too, when he was thinking. "Not sure. Instinct? I'm basically a walking weapon, Od. Clue's in the name: *War*suit. I'm designed to adopt aggressive tactics, unless my pilot specifies otherwise."

Od could see the logic in this, although he didn't like it.

"Well, I'm specifying otherwise," he said. "Let's keep the death and carnage to a minimum if we can. Call it the John Connor rule."

"The what?"

"You've seen *Terminator 2*."

"No, I haven't."

"Yes, you have. We watched it together. Oh no. Wait." Od was forgetting that, just because Wes sounded and acted like his father, it didn't mean he *was* his father. They didn't share all of the same experiences and memories. "Never mind."

"All right, I'm in the lock now. Bypassing the security protocols. And... done. Open sesame."

Ahead, the door yawned wide. Through its frame Od could see the soldier who was dressed like a tramp, standing with pistol drawn. The soldier's jaw dropped as he caught his first glimpse of the metal behemoth lumbering towards him from the gloom of the tunnel. Apparently he had no idea what he'd been helping to guard all this time.

"Can I talk to him?" said Od.

"Engaging external speakers."

"You need to move," Od said to the soldier. His voice boomed down the tunnel, and the soldier looked more alarmed and awestruck than ever.

"Seriously," said Od. Warsuit 1.0 was now less than twenty metres from the exit. "I'm coming through, and there's a bunch of bad guys not far behind. You need to start running *now*."

The soldier dithered, then decided. Warsuit 1.0 was rushing at him like an oncoming train. He turned tail and fled through the pair of outer doors. A moment later, Warsuit 1.0 barged into the prefab unit and smashed straight through the opposite wall. The prefab shattered in an explosion of plywood and plasterboard. The fake hut around it likewise was reduced to tinder. Warsuit 1.0 skidded to a halt on the floor of the quarry, covered in dust and debris.

"We made it," breathed Od. "Awesome."

"Let's not pat ourselves on the back just yet," said Wes. "We still have a dozen T-Cellers on our tail. Quarter of a minute before they catch up with us. Perhaps we should reconsider engaging them...?"

"Or," said Od, "we simply shut the door on them."

"No can do. The door's on a hardwired, isolated timer mechanism which I have no way of overriding. It closes automatically forty seconds after opening, but not before then."

"Well, so what? They can't harm us."

"But they can harm him." Wes flagged up the tramp-soldier on a screen. The man, a faint figure in the grey early-dawn light, was halfway across the quarry but had stopped running. He gawped at Warsuit 1.0. He couldn't seem to tear his gaze off it.

"You'd think he'd never seen a seven-metre-tall Warsuit before," said Od.

"Quite," said Wes. "Here they come, Od. What do we do? I've already target-acquired the first three of them. Single shots to the head. We could have them on the ground in less than a second. Just give the word."

"There – there must be something else we can do," Od said in desperation. "Surely."

The T-Cell operatives were all out in the open, past the shambles of the prefab, and already they had spotted the tramp-soldier nearby. The gun in his hand marked him out as an enemy combatant, even if the rags he was wearing didn't. Several of the T-Cellers turned their wave cannons on him.

"They'll shoot him, Od. I need a decision. Make up your mind. Quick."

It was agonising. Od had no desire to kill anyone. More than that, he just didn't have the capacity to do it. It wasn't in his mental make-up. He'd played his fair share of shoot-'em-ups, of course, eliminating thousands of zombies and Nazis and the like, and never had a problem with that.

But this was no videogame. This was the real deal. He would be responsible for ending real lives, creating real corpses.

Set against that, a man's life was at stake. The soldier was in mortal danger, unless Od acted.

Crosshairs were superimposed on more and more of the T-Cellers' heads, deadly green haloes.

"Use non-lethal force," Od said. "John Connor rule, remember."

"Shoot to wound?" said Wes. "All right, but I should warn you, it won't guarantee that man's safety."

"Do it anyway."

Od lifted his right arm and Wes rotated the gun barrels till the second smallest was uppermost. Onscreen, the crosshairs moved, latching onto other parts of the T-Cellers' bodies than their heads: knees, elbows, thighs, shoulders.

"Selecting armour-piercing rounds. With all that polyethylene bulletproofing on them, we have to make sure."

"Understood. Fire!"

Bullets sprayed from Warsuit 1.0's arm with lightning speed and pinpoint precision. Every single shot found its mark, flawlessly accurate. Down went the T-Cellers, one after another, like a row of tin ducks at a fairground shooting gallery. In next to no time, all of them were sprawled on the quarry floor, clutching wounds, writhing. They were in too much pain even to think about picking up their wave cannons again.

Watching them, Od felt distinctly queasy. But he knew he had made the best choice under the circumstances.

"They'll live, right?" he asked Wes.

"They will. Some of them might never walk properly again, mind."

"Let's take out their guns for good measure. Just in case."

Wes targeted the wave cannons the T-Cellers had dropped, blasting each to bits where it lay on the ground.

The tramp-soldier looked stunned but grateful, like someone who could hardly believe his luck. He offered Warsuit 1.0 a tentative salute. Then, pistol raised, he went over to the T-Cellers. He didn't move like a tramp any more.

"All right, you lot," he growled, pointing the gun at them. "Try anything funny, and I won't be anywhere near as merciful as whoever's inside that real-life Transformer robot just was."

The T-Cellers who could raise their arms in surrender, did.

Inside the Warsuit, Wes made a thoughtful, back-of-the-throat noise. "Ah, now look at this. This is interesting."

"What?" said Od.

"I'm picking up aircraft radar signatures. Helicopters, three of them, inbound. Zeroing in on our location."

"More T-Cell people?"

"No. The helicopters are Chinooks. British military troop transport. Reinforcements, I assume. They've been scrambled from the base over at Carnforth and they've come to take back Selston Tor."

"Well, that's good news."

"Indeed. However..."

"There's bad news as well," Od said with a groan.

"Afraid so. T-Cell have their own air transport. Just the one. And it's taken off from the installation and is headed this way."

"What sort of aircraft is it?"

"That sort," said Wes.

On the main screen a large, intimidating-looking silver gunship appeared above the rim of the quarry. It hovered on the thrust generated by six downward-pointing jet propulsion units. It was crescent-shaped, the tips of its curved wings almost touching at the front like a crab's pincers. On top was a cockpit canopy, a blister of glass with the flight crew inside. From its belly and the underside of its wings a number of pods and launch tubes hung – a bristling array of weapons.

The gunship was turning head-on towards Warsuit 1.0, with obvious hostile intent.

Chapter 10

"They've locked on to us," said Wes. "I'm being 'painted' with multiple laser target designators. The crew's radioed their base. They're requesting permission to proceed."

"Proceed with opening fire on us, you mean?"

"And that's a pretty serious-looking payload they're carrying. Enough to do some damage even to me."

"Oh God," said Od, fighting down panic. "Why? I don't get this at all. First they want to steal you, now they want to destroy you?"

"Listen in."

Wes relayed the T-Cellers' radio conversation over the loudspeaker.

"... repeat, we have the objective in our sights, sir. The Warsuit is at our mercy." This was the gunship's captain talking.

"And there's absolutely no alternative?" drawled a deep, aristocratic voice. It spoke with the suave self-assurance of someone who had known all his life that he was born to lead and give orders. "No way we can acquire it in one piece now?"

"That's a negative, Mr d'Arc. Somebody got to the suit before we did. I don't understand how, because there wasn't supposed to be anybody in that lab. But, whoever it is, they've already shown aggressive behaviour. They took out the entire strike team."

"I'm aware of that, Hexaflyer Bravo Tango. I've been following the action via the live feeds from their helmet cams. Frankly, those men got what they deserved for their incompetence. And mark my words, it won't be their only punishment."

The man called d'Arc heaved a world-weary sigh.

"Well, if T-Cell can't have the suit, I don't see why anyone else should either. Besides, we have the brains behind the whole project staying as our guest here. We just have to persuade him to co-operate with us. Then all our problems are solved."

"Dad," Od murmured. "That's Dad he's talking about."

"I think you're right," said Wes.

"So by all means," continued d'Arc, "obliterate

the Warsuit. Leave nothing of it behind, not so much as a single rivet. Reduce it to slag."

"Roger that, sir."

"And Hexaflyer Bravo Tango? Don't mess up. One fiasco is more than enough for one night."

"Yes, sir," said the gunship captain with an audible gulp. "Hexaflyer Bravo Tango over and out."

"They're priming missiles, Od," said Wes. "Hi-ex warheads. We have less than five seconds."

"Get us out of here!" Od yelled.

"Routing power to main thrusters. Lift-off in three, two, one..."

Warsuit 1.0 began to roar and shake violently. At once, Od felt an incredible pressure bearing down on him from above. It was as if someone had thrown an invisible tarpaulin over him and was pulling down hard on the corners. He seemed to have doubled in weight. Just keeping his head up took a supreme effort, the muscles in his neck aching with the strain. He tried to scream but even his voice had become too heavy and the cry remained trapped in his throat.

His vision was a blur but he could just make out the screen images. They leapt about crazily. Landscape and sky competed to see which could take up more screen space.

Then, just when Od was beginning to think he couldn't stand it any longer, things calmed a bit. The roar lessened. The shaking got smoother. There was a sensation of bumpy, energetic progress, like being in a car riding over a gravel driveway full of potholes.

On the main screen he saw the moors gliding by below. Roads glimmered in the dim pearly grey light, narrow as pencil strokes. Trees were tiny asterisks. Here and there was a house, no bigger than a Tetris block.

"Flying," he said softly. "We're actually flying."

"Yes," said Wes. "Sorry about the acceleration. Hope the g-force wasn't too unpleasant. I had to use maximum thrust. Otherwise we'd be nothing but wreckage right now."

"Flying," repeated Od. He didn't know whether he was terrified or exhilarated. It was a bit of both, he decided.

"We're travelling at four hundred miles per hour, cruising at an altitude of five thousand feet. You're quite safe. Nothing to worry about. I've put a good distance between us and that gunship, that Hexaflyer thing, and even if it tries to catch up, the Warsuit has a radar cross-section of almost zero. As an added precaution I'm elevating into that cloud layer ahead.

We'll be invisible to both electronic detection and the naked eye."

Od almost said, "Flying," a third time. But then his phone sang its ringtone, the chorus of Green Day's "Know Your Enemy".

"You have an incoming call," Wes said.

"Yeah. Nothing I can do about it. Kind of hard to reach my phone at the moment."

"I can help."

A large version of his phone's display appeared on a screen in front of Od. UNKNOWN CALLER, it said.

"You want to take it?" Wes asked.

"I'm five thousand feet above the ground in a one-person, man-shaped aircraft. Of course I've got time to chat."

Even as he delivered the quip, Od had a sudden sneaking suspicion that he knew who was trying to get in touch with him. He was about to tell Wes to cut the connection, but by then it was too late.

Sure enough, it was as he feared.

Her. Angelica W-K.

"Od," she said, frostily serene, like an iceberg on a collision course with an ocean liner. "I imagine you're feeling rather pleased with yourself."

"I wouldn't say pleased. A little airsick, maybe."

"Clever, the way you gave us the slip back at the house. Not so clever, breaking into Selston Tor. Do you have any idea how much trouble you're in?"

"From your tone of voice, I'm guessing it's a lot."

"You have stolen – that's the only word for it – *stolen* an item of government property worth a billion pounds."

"You're kidding!" This was said with frank astonishment.

"One point two billion, to be precise," said Angelica W-K. "For that serious a crime, I don't think there's a jail sentence long enough. When you're caught, young man, they won't simply lock you up and throw away the key. They'll forget where they put you. You won't see the light of day again until you're ninety, and maybe not even then."

Od felt a sudden, swooping sense of dread as the full impact of what he'd done hit home. He began to tremble, and his stomach knotted so tightly he thought it might just suck him into himself like a black hole. He felt close to throwing up, which in the limited confines of the Warsuit would have been even less pleasant than throwing up usually was.

Then his father's advice about Angelica W-K came back to him. *Treat her as you would a dangerous dog. A blonde, sexy, dangerous dog*. In his mind's eye Od saw again that absurd, comedy image of a lipsticked Rottweiler. It calmed him a little, just enough.

What did you do when confronted by a dangerous dog? You made sure not to show fear.

"I take your point, Miss W-K," he said. "When you put it like that, I have been a bit of an ASBO kid, haven't I? But look at it another way. If I hadn't taken Warsuit One Point Oh out of Selston Tor when I did, who would have it right now? I'll tell you. T-Cell, that's who. So, instead of stealing a billion quid's worth of government property, I've actually kept it from falling into enemy hands. You should be thanking me, not threatening me."

A brief pause from Angelica W-K's end of the line told him all he needed to know. He was right, and she knew it. She just didn't care to admit it.

"That may be so," she said stiffly. "But it doesn't change the fact that you've made off with the Warsuit and we want it back. So here's what we're going to do. We're going to arrange a rendezvous. We meet up, you hand over the suit, and I guarantee that'll be the end of the matter. There'll be no repercussions for you, no being taken into custody, no criminal prosecution. You walk away scot-free. I'm being more than generous here, under the circumstances."

"It's a very tempting offer. But I'm going to have to say no."

"That would be highly unwise. I'm giving you this one chance, and one chance only. Return the suit. It'll be the best outcome for all of us."

"No."

Od found it weirdly exhilarating to defy Angelica W-K like this. He wasn't just standing up to her, he was standing up to everything she represented – the forces of authority, the powers-that-be, the big people who pushed the little people around. "Not yet. You can have it back but not till after I'm done with it. I heard that posh bloke, d'Arc, say they're going to try and persuade my dad to work for them."

"You know about Jupiter d'Arc?"

"I know he's got a stupid name and an accent like Prince Charles. I can also tell he's ruthless, so I reckon being 'persuaded' won't be much fun for my dad. It'll probably involve torture, sleep deprivation, beating up... You know, the sort of stuff you lot do to terror suspects to get them to confess."

"Oh how very worldly wise you are, Od. How very

flippant, too. Don't forget you're talking about such things happening your father. Not so funny when it's a close relative, eh?"

"I'm not trying to be funny, as a matter of fact. I'm scared as hell for my dad. But at least I know it doesn't have to happen to him, because I can stop it. I have exactly what I need to prevent it. This big hunk of tin I'm in."

Wes gave a soft, polite cough. "'Big hunk of tin'?"

"No offence," Od said.

"I'm not offended," said Angelica W-K.

"I was talking to the suit, not you."

"Ah yes, the suit. You know that the Warsuit is still in the early stages of production, don't you? It is, after all, just version one point oh."

Od sensed that Angelica W-K was taking a fresh tack, trying to worm through his defences another way.

"It hasn't been field-tested. It's months away from being certified combat-ready. You're on board something that could malfunction at any moment. What if the operating system freezes, just like that, while you're in mid-air? You'd drop like a stone. Think about it."

As if to underscore her point, the suit began to

shudder and vibrate around Od. His breath caught.

"Nothing to worry about," Wes reassured him. "Just a patch of turbulence. Air pocket. Be through it in a moment."

"My dad built this thing," Od said to Angelica W-K as the turbulence subsided. "He knows his stuff. I'm sure he's put in failsafes and backups by the bucketload. He wouldn't have let me near the suit if he didn't think it was a hundred per cent safe."

"I hate to be the one to break it to you, Od, but your father isn't all that you think he is. You have this impression of him as a crackpot genius, and he is, but crackpot is another way of saying unreliable. In all my dealings with him, I've found him obstructive, difficult, sometimes even downright infuriating."

"That probably says more about you than about him."

"He's putting you in terrible danger, don't you see?" She sounded concerned, on the surface. Beneath, though, anger still bubbled and simmered. "What kind of father would do that to his son? He's thinking only about himself, not you. His own selfish needs."

"It's hardly selfish to want to be rescued from terrorists. I'd call it common sense."

"At the risk of his only child's life?"

"It's a risk I'm prepared to take. Do you have parents, Miss W-K? What am I saying? Of course you don't. You were brewed in a test tube in a government laboratory, weren't you?"

Angelica W-K spluttered.

"Me," Od continued, "I don't have a mum any more, but I do still have a dad, and as he's the only parent I've got, in fact the only family, I'm going to do my very best to keep him. And if that means putting myself in harm's way, then OK, that's just how it has to be."

He meant every word he said. Angelica W-K was just trying to sow doubt in his mind, make him question his father's character and motives. He wouldn't let her succeed.

What was it his dad had said? *This woman will do anything to get her own way.* Well, not this time, lady.

"Your mother," Angelica W-K said. "Hmmm. Funny you should mention her. I wasn't going to go there, but..."

"No, you can go there," Od said, pretending to be reasonable. "Be my guest. Say what you like about my dead mother. Slag her off if you like. Because that'll just make me even more annoyed with you and I'll find it a whole lot easier telling you to get stuffed."

"It wasn't cancer that killed her, you know."

"Oh yes it was," Od replied hotly. "Don't talk rubbish. I saw the brain scans. I watched her with my own eyes, wasting away day by day. She had a tumour in her head the size of an orange, and it slowly ate her alive."

"She had cancer, yes. I'm not denying that. But the surgery she had should have saved her."

"*Could* have," said Od. "We were told it would be fifty-fifty. The operation was as likely to kill her as cure her. Like a coin toss, heads or tails. She knew that going in. We all did. It was a gamble she was willing to take. *Had* to take. The tumour was right next to her brain stem. A malignant glioma, it's called. And if the surgeon made the tiniest mistake, slipped up by even a millimetre, that would be it. End of story.

"And he did. It sucks, but he did. She lost the coin toss. At least we were warned in advance what the odds were. Dad and I said our goodbyes to her before she went under the anaesthetic, just in case. At least we had that."

"You were told an error happened," said Angelica W-K. Her tone was cordially vicious. "That's the official account of events. The truth is different."

"The truth?"

"It was a specialist hospital where she was treated, wasn't it? A place called the Oncodyne Clinic. The surgery was a highly advanced procedure. Experimental. Cutting-edge."

"Something to do with ion beams fired by a laser, I think. So? Standard radiation therapy hadn't worked. Ordinary scalpel-type surgery wouldn't have had a chance. It was her only hope."

"Yet I know for a fact that the surgeon, the entire medical team, did everything right. What went wrong was beyond their control."

"I don't want to hear this," Od said. "I don't want to hear any of it."

"I think you need to, Od."

"No, I don't. You can shut up now."

"Why are scared of the truth?"

"Because it isn't the truth. Nothing that comes out of your big fat lying gob is the truth."

"I swear I'm not lying."

"I said shut up."

"Your father knows what really happened, why she

died." There was an almost gleeful note in Angelica W-K's voice now. "Of course, I'd never accuse him of being responsible for her death. But haven't you wondered why he's been so withdrawn since then, so obsessive? It's as if he's trying to make up for what happened. As if he feels guilty somehow."

"Not listening."

"Ask him yourself, then. Ask him why he made the Warsuit."

"All right, I will," said Od. "Right after I've got him out of T-Cell's clutches. Now, you're starting to bore me. I'm ending the conversation."

"Od, hear me out. You have no idea what you're up against." She was giving it one last, desperate shot. "I've been fighting people like T-Cell my whole professional life. They're beyond dangerous. They're great white sharks in human form. They kill to live and live to kill. What are you going to do, anyway? You don't even know how to find your father. You have no idea where he is."

"Do you?"

"No. We assume T-Cell must have a base of operations somewhere, but we've never been able to pinpoint its location."

"Then we're all in the same boat," said Od. "Only

difference is, I've got an oar and you don't. Goodbye, Miss W-K. See ya, wouldn't want to be ya."

"Od!"

"Wes, cut her off, will you?"

CALL ENDED appeared on the screen.

"Done," said Wes.

"And can you block any further incoming calls from that same number?"

"One moment. Also done."

"Thanks."

"Od..."

"Hold on. Give me a second."

Od collected his thoughts. He had just put himself firmly on the wrong side of Angelica W-K. That didn't bother him on a personal level. On a practical level, though, it wasn't the smartest of moves. She was a woman with power and clout, and the type to hold a grudge, too. She could seriously mess up his life if she felt like it, and right now she probably did feel like it.

Oh well, he'd just have to deal with that when he came to it.

What troubled him more were the dark hints she had dropped about his mother's death. Had she been making it all up? If so, why? To rattle him, perhaps.

Cause him to second-guess himself. Drive a wedge between him and his father and deter him from his rescue mission. Would Angelica W-K stoop so low as to use the death of someone's parent in order to put the thumbscrews on that person? Oh yes, Od felt sure she would.

At the same time, something she'd said did chime with his own feelings about his father.

Haven't you wondered why he's been so withdrawn since then, so obsessive? It's as if he's trying to make up for what happened. As if he feels guilty somehow.

Tremaine Fitch had been a changed man since losing his wife. Which was only to be expected. He had loved her very much. She had died tragically young, long before she should have. That kind of grief was particularly hard to bear.

But he hadn't become merely sad. He had become, deep in the heart of himself, stone cold. Outwardly he could still be witty, jolly, affectionate, warm. But a hollowness had settled in his soul. A bitterness. Od had seen it on those days when his father would simply sit and stare at nothing, his mouth set hard.

He had started working at Selston Tor a mere two months after the funeral. He had uprooted himself and Od from all they knew and were used to. He had dragged them hundreds of miles across the country, away from the university town where he had been a lecturer and research fellow and Od had had friends and attended a good school and been doing well, coming top in his year in almost every subject. He had relocated them to the dreary moors, a place where the skies were constantly overcast and nothing of any importance happened.

In a brooding landscape, Tremaine Fitch had brooded. In a place of distances, he had become distant.

And all along, at the nuclear research installation that wasn't really a nuclear research installation, he had been hard at work building Warsuit 1.0. He had thrown himself, heart and soul, into the project. He had given it his all.

Making a war machine that was uniquely powerful and lethal.

Out of anger? A desire for revenge? Hatred for a world that had robbed him of his true love?

"Od?"

"Yeah, Wes?"

"I've no wish to intrude, but you may like to know that I've picked up the Hexaflyer's radar signature again. It's approximately fifty miles south of us, bearing due west. It's travelling at a fair old lick, just sub-Mach. I think we can safely assume it's returning to base, wherever base is."

"Can we follow it?"

"I'm already plotting a flight path to intercept."

"They've got to be going where Dad is."

"It's likely, isn't it? It's a lead, at any rate."

Od felt the Warsuit tip to the left as Wes altered course.

His head was full of misgivings and suspicions.

His heart, by contrast, was empty of everything but certainty.

CHAPTER 11

Within minutes Warsuit 1.0 was behind Hexaflyer Bravo Tango, matching its course and its groundspeed of 650 mph but keeping a good distance between them. They had left the coast of Britain behind and were over the Atlantic. The ocean, illuminated by a breathtaking sunrise, glittered gold, ruby and sapphire, a blanket of treasures.

Od wasn't in the mood for appreciating the view, however. All his attention was focused on the far-off dot on the horizon that was the T-Cell gunship. He wondered what its destination was, where it was leading him to out in this vast desert of seawater.

"There are no islands anywhere around here." Wes illustrated the remark by putting a map up on a screen. Blue, blue, nothing but blue. "The Azores and the Canaries will pass well to the south of us if we maintain this heading, and that thing doesn't look to me like it has the fuel capacity to go all the way to north America. It'd need to be a lot larger."

"Maybe this is a suicide run," said Od. "They didn't manage to capture or destroy the suit, and they'd rather kill themselves than go back and face the wrath of Jupiter d'Arc."

Wes chuckled.

"I'm only half joking."

"I know."

"D'Arc," Od mused. "That can't be his real name, can it? As in night-time? No light? It sounds like a magician's stage name."

"You're thinking it's spelled D-A-R-K."

"Isn't it?"

"No. D-apostrophe-A-R-C. Same as Jeanne d'Arc – Joan of Arc."

"Ohhh. Don't suppose he's a descendant of hers."

"Maybe."

"He doesn't have a French accent, though. Do we know anything about him at all?"

"Let me dig around in a couple of databases," said Wes. "Precious little coming up. I've got a date of birth. December the twenty-fifth, 1965. That's unfortunate timing, Birthday and Christmas on the same day. Born and raised in London, resident there till 1987. After that, nothing. He drops off the grid entirely."

"Any family?"

"Just parents. Both killed in a house fire. That was in 1987 too, not long before he disappeared. Police suspected arson but nothing was proved. D'Arc himself was away at university at the time, so it can't have been him who set the fire, if that's what you're thinking. His alibi is cast-iron."

"So for a quarter of a century the guy's been an invisible man," said Od. "Hc hasn't officially existed."

"No bank accounts. No driving licence. Not a trace of him anywhere in the system. No internet presence. He hasn't had so much as a parking ticket."

"Facebook page, surely."

Wes laughed. "As if."

"How do you *do* that nowadays? Vanish? Everybody leaves an electronic paper-trail. It's just not feasible."

"Yet somehow he's managed it, and in the meantime become head honcho at T-Cell."

"Should we be impressed?"

"I think maybe we should, a little."

"What about T-Cell itself? What's their game?"

"Again, I'm drawing almost a complete blank," said Wes. "Every scrap of information the government has on them is Restricted Access. Highly classified stuff, stored behind brick-thick firewalls and massively encrypted. I could probably plough my way through, given a day or so, but really, the levels of security are fortress-like. It's all I can do just to lurk at the edges without tripping any of a dozen intruder alarms. The public, clearly, is not supposed to ever hear about T-Cell."

"The bare bones. Snippets. Anything. I need some idea of what we're facing."

"They've been operating for a little over a decade, that I can tell you," said Wes. "They claim to have peaceful intentions. Their objective is the liberation of technology. They're against the suppression of inventions and scientific advances that can improve the state of humankind. I'm getting this from a manifesto posted on some ancient, forgotten website that everyone else appears to have overlooked. The location is so obscure, most search engines give it a four-oh-four Not Found error code."

"You're saying they're idealists. They want all technology to be shared fairly among the masses."

"More or less."

"Funny way of going about it. They shot those soldiers and tried to blow up this suit and me with it. I mean, what's idealistic about that?"

"They regard themselves as freedom fighters. Anything's justified if you feel your cause is just. Even murder. The name T-Cell..."

"I recognise the word," said Od. "From my mum's cancer. The doctors were always going on about her 'T-cell count' being high or low or whatever. T-cells are lymphocytes, white blood cells, part of the body's immune system. They help fight viruses and such."

"And T-Cell, the organisation, believe there's a disease at the heart of society, a sickness that it's their sworn duty to combat and defeat. By whatever means necessary."

"Nice. So they're not just fanatics, they're delusional fanatics. And these are the people who've nabbed Dad. They're not going to give him back if we just ask nicely, are they?"

"I suspect it'll take a bit more than 'please' and 'thank you'."

"Bunch of lousy..." Od let loose with some juicy words to describe his feelings about T-Cell.

"Language!" Wes scolded.

"Oi, just because you talk like my father, doesn't mean you have to act like him as well."

"Sorry, Od. Can't help myself. It's just one of the subroutines Professor Fitch installed."

"Well, can it be uninstalled?"

"Let's see. Yes. Proceed?"

"Picture me hitting the Enter key." Od swore again, experimentally. There was no reaction from Wes. He grinned. "Hey, I've just customised you."

"And you're welcome to keep the customisations coming," said Wes. "It's my job to adapt my functions to my pilot's personality and habits. The smoother the interface between pilot and suit, the more effective we are as a team."

A team.

Od had never considered himself a team player. In school sports, he could barely summon up the enthusiasm to take part. Football, athletics, cricket, you name it, he would loiter on the sidelines and involve himself as little as he could without the teacher noticing. Even online, in multi-player games, he seldom hooked up with other people's bands of roaming avatars. He kept aloof in the digital world as well as the actual. He didn't necessarily prefer it that way. It just seemed to be the role he was fated for.

But now...?

"Hexaflyer Bravo Tango has started to descend," Wes informed him. "If I didn't know better, I'd say it was getting ready to land."

"But there's nowhere *to* land," said Od, scanning the empty seascape around them. "Unless it's going underwater. Is it amphibious?"

"With those jets? Unlikely. Your suicide run theory's looking more and more plausible."

"I don't suppose you're getting any clues from their comms."

"None. The crew are observing complete radio silence."

"Hey, what's that?" Od had spied a disturbance in the water's surface, a speck of white amid the endless blue. "See? There. Dead ahead."

"Magnifying," said Wes. "Zooming in. Enhancing resolution."

The image enlarged in stages, blurring then sharpening with each leap of magnification. The whiteness had a distinct spiral shape, like a galaxy, and it was steadily spreading and deepening.

"A...whirlpool?" said Od, bemused.

"No other word for it."

"This isn't just some random phenomenon. Can't

be. It must be manmade."

"Agreed. And the Hexaflyer's making a beeline for it."

The whirlpool grew bigger and still bigger. Soon it was at least a hundred metres across, and revolving at dizzying speed. A perfect round hole had yawned in the ocean, and at its heart a glistening, water-walled shaft tunnelled straight down.

Hexaflyer Bravo Tango came to a halt directly above this huge vortex, suspending itself on six jets of air. Its propulsion units revolved in sequence, turning upside down. Then it shot vertically downwards, plunging into the whirlpool's maw.

"Follow?" asked Wes.

"I think we have to. They'll get away from us if we don't. Keep your distance, though. Don't want to get spotted."

Warsuit 1.0 went into a steep swoop, diving head first towards the liquid vortex.

What lay in store below? What was the Hexaflyer heading for? Was the Warsuit even watertight?

These and other questions crowded into Od's brain.

No point wondering. He'd find out soon enough.

CHAPTER 12

The Warsuit shuddered and jolted as it entered the maelstrom. Winds whipped up by the whirlpool's revolutions pummelled the suit. Ropes of water snaked out from the whirlpool's sides and lashed it violently. The roar of swirling, churning ocean was tremendous. Even cocooned within his metal shell, Od was deafened. The noise was so loud it almost drowned his thoughts. Hanging upside down, with the blood rushing to his head, he focused on the sleek silver Hexaflyer far below. The T-Cell gunship, with its thirty-metre wingspan, was bigger and heavier than Warsuit 1.0. Its crew had evidently made this trip into the whirlpool before. If they could manage it safely, Od reasoned, so could the Warsuit.

Several metres below the surface the Warsuit passed through a gigantic metal hoop. Bladeless suction fans within the hoop were responsible for the titanic centrifugal forces generating the whirlpool. A second, narrower hoop, connected to the first by huge, sturdy cables, was situated a short way further down. There was a third below that, its diameter smaller still, and a fourth. Od could see the hoops descending into the darkness of the depths. Each was playing its part in creating the vortex, this watery gateway to somewhere.

Way down at the whirlpool's base Od glimpsed a vast shadow.

"What *is* that?" He had to shout to be heard over the whirlpool's turmoil. "Is it one of those ocean trenches?"

"No," Wes replied. "The seabed is much further down. Whatever that is, it has mass. Some kind of vessel. I'm registering engine noise – propeller cavitation – and heat from a nuclear power source."

"But it looks like it's about a mile long."

"I know. I keep thinking my sensors must be misreading. But they're not."

"You're telling me someone's built a submarine *one mile long*?"

"I'm telling you that's the only thing it can be. And look."

A circle of brightness had opened up at the bottom of the whirlpool. The Hexaflyer was briefly silhouetted against it like a bat against the moon, and then the brightness swallowed the gunship up. A second later, the circle began to narrow on either side, like some kind of double eclipse.

"A hatch," said Wes. "The Hexaflyer's gone in."

"Then so should we," Od said with resolve. At that moment he became aware of a kind of weird, sinking, groaning sound. "What's that?"

"The hoops. Their mechanisms are shutting down."

"But if they're shutting down, that means..."

"The whirlpool's going to shut down too."

"Move!"

Warsuit 1.0 poured on speed. The massive cables that joined the hoops together were reeling them swiftly downwards to the submarine. Meanwhile the walls of the whirlpool were losing shape, becoming sloppier, less stable. Sheets of water began cascading from above like storm rain, hammering down on the suit. One screen showed that the hole at the top of the whirlpool had sealed itself, shutting out the distant bright dot of sky. Bit by bit, downwards, the rest of the vortex was doing the same, closing, like a wound healing.

And, below, the hatch itself was very nearly shut.

"Hurry!" Od urged Wes.

Thrusters flaring, Warsuit 1.0 accelerated even faster. The second hoop was now firmly nestled within the top hoop, and both of those were closing in on the third hoop down. The Warsuit was racing to beat them to the sub. The cone of air around it was rapidly shrinking. A readout gauge told Od that they were at a depth of 550 fathoms. Once the whirlpool dissolved completely, the suit would be submerged a kilometre below the surface.

He didn't know whether it could survive the crushing pressures so far down, and he wouldn't have asked Wes even if there'd been time to. He had a feeling the answer would be not the one he was hoping for.

The first three hoops were fitted snugly together and drawing almost level with the fourth. There was hardly any of the whirlpool left, just a small pocket of air that was shrinking fast, the water around it rotating only through its own inertia.

The gap between the hatch doors was reduced to just a sliver. It looked like the Warsuit wasn't going to make it. Od held his breath and gritted his teeth and prayed.

Then – *bump, scrape* – the Warsuit slid between the doors, with barely a millimetre to spare on either side. The hatch closed tight shut. Next instant, water slammed down onto the doors with a tumultuous *WHUMP* as the whirlpool finally imploded and cancelled itself out of existence, becoming nothing but a sizzling froth of bubbles.

Od let out a whoop of triumph. Wes, meanwhile, braked and turned the right way up using various different thrusters. Warsuit 1.0 came to rest gently on its feet on a broad metal catwalk.

Once Od's heart rate had calmed to normal – it had been the narrowest of narrow squeaks – he took stock of his surroundings. The screens showed floors descending in tiers, like layers of a cake. Hexaflyers were parked on several of them, alongside other aircraft the likes of which Od had never seen. There were things that resembled helicopters but were knife-thin and had room in their cockpits for just a single crew member. There were planes that put him in mind of a Harrier jump jet spliced with a Challenger tank. There were even disc-shaped craft very reminiscent of UFOs.

He was in a hangar full of, it seemed, sci-fi movie flying machines.

"Whoa," he said. "This is – "

"Odysseus Fitch!"

The voice came from outside. Od had heard it before, just the once. He recognised it only too well.

A tall man was standing at the end of the catwalk. He wore a tailored double-breasted suit and had immaculate, side-swept hair. He carried himself with an air of swaggering authority, one hand in jacket pocket, nose ever so slightly up-turned. His smile was wide and welcoming and, to Od's eyes, supremely false.

"That is you in there, isn't it, Odysseus?" the man continued. "Please allow me to introduce myself. The name's Jupiter d'Arc."

Immediately Od raised his right arm. Wes obligingly selected a medium-sized barrel.

"Come, come," said d'Arc. "There's no call for such belligerent posturing. Look at me." He spread out his hands. "I'm unarmed. I'm no threat to you. I come in peace."

Od's reply was to have Wes ratchet the barrels round to the next largest in calibre.

"Very well, young man. I take the point. Quite a specimen of military hardware you've got there. I behold and marvel. And, really, how thoughtful of you to bring it to me. Delivering it right to my doorstep, so to speak. You've saved me a great deal of time and trouble. Here I was thinking you'd never be so unwary as to fall for my trap, and yet you did. Hook, line and sinker."

"Trap?" said Od to Wes. "We shadowed the Hexaflyer the whole way here. The crew had no idea there was anyone following them. He's just trying to make out that I'm stupid and he's smart, that's all. Right?"

"I instructed Hexaflyer Bravo Tango to act as a lure," d'Arc explained. "I had it dangle itself in front of your nose, knowing you'd be unable to resist taking the bait. The crew did their jobs perfectly. They've more than redeemed themselves for missing their chance to eliminate you in that quarry."

"Come to think of it," Wes said, "it did seem a bit convenient, the Hexaflyer coming into radar range like that. But the fact remains that we're here now, face to face with d'Arc, and we have a Warsuit and he doesn't."

"Good point." To d'Arc, over the external speaker, Od said, "All right, you got me. It was a cunning trick and I fell for it. So what? Doesn't change anything as far as I'm concerned. I've come for Professor Fitch.

I want him back, and I'll do whatever it takes to get him."

"You mean your father."

"Yes," Od sighed, "my father. Bring him here now, or else."

"Or else what?" said d'Arc. "You'll vaporise me where I stand? I think not. You've already shown a reluctance to take life. You don't have it in you."

"OK then." Od turned, aiming the Warsuit's arm out over the catwalk handrail. "All these cool-looking aircraft of yours? Worth a few quid, I'd say. How about I start lobbing missiles at them? I bet there'd be some spectacular fireworks."

"You could, I suppose." If d'Arc was in the least bit worried or intimidated, he gave no sign. If anything, he seemed faintly bored. "I'd advise against it, though. Don't forget we're in a submersible vehicle some considerable distance underwater. You start blowing things up willy-nilly, who knows what might happen? A chain reaction, perhaps. A series of explosions of unstoppable momentum that will punch a hole in this vessel's shell and doom us all. You wouldn't want that, would you? Especially not with dear old Daddy aboard. What if I propose a simpler alternative?"

D'Arc snapped his fingers and two grey-suited T-Cell operatives emerged from behind a nearby bulkhead. They marched onto the catwalk supporting a third figure between them, a man in civilian clothing who staggered along, tripping over his own feet. Od quickly saw why. The man's head was covered in a linen sack. He couldn't see where he was going.

Halting beside d'Arc, one of the T-Cell paramilitaries tugged the sack off, and there stood Od's father.

He blinked dazedly around. Then his gaze fell on Warsuit 1.0 and, with an expression that was both glad and rueful, he nodded.

"Dad," said Od, feeling a terrific rush of relief.

"Well done, son," said Professor Tremaine Fitch. He looked unharmed. Haggard, exhausted, somewhat wobbly on his legs, but basically OK. "Good work. You did everything I asked. Only, now I wish you hadn't. Not your fault, but when I set things up for you to take the suit and come after me, I had no idea just how demented these people are."

"Demented?" said d'Arc. "No. Determined, maybe. Willing to take extreme measures. But not demented."

"What's he talking about?" Od asked Wes. "There's something here I'm not seeing."

"I think I am," said Wes. "I'm running a thermal image scan of your father. There's something inside him, a foreign object of some sort."

Od's father's body was displayed onscreen in a spectrum of colours, showing the hotter and cooler parts of him. Wes zoomed in on his head. Where Tremaine Fitch's skull met his spine, amid warm reds and yellows, a tiny blue oblong stood out in sharp contrast.

"It's inorganic," Wes said. "The casing is plastic and silicon. Inside there's a substance, some sort of resinous compound I can't identify."

At a gesture from d'Arc, the two T-Cell operatives shoved Tremaine Fitch to his knees. One of them forced him to turn his head, exposing a small bandage on the side of his neck.

"We," said d'Arc, "have taken the liberty of carrying out a minor surgical procedure on your father, Odysseus. Nothing too traumatic. It was done under a local anaesthetic. Quite painless, I'm assured."

"What is it?" Od said menacingly. "What have you put in his head?"

"You can't tell from your thermal image? We've implanted a capsule containing a few milligrammes of PETN, an ultra high explosive. The capsule has a remote detonator the size of a pinhead attached to it. And, oh look, here's the transmitter trigger."

D'Arc undid a couple of shirt buttons to reveal a small black plastic rectangle attached to his chest. It reminded Od of the key fob you use to unlock a car electronically. A tiny red diode winked in the very centre of it.

"The trigger is synched to my heartbeat," the T-Cell leader went on. "As long as I continue to have a detectable pulse, the transmitter will continue beaming a suppression command to the detonator. Should for any reason my heart stop... Well, you can work out the rest."

Od let out a growl.

"Yes, surely this is the very definition of irony," said d'Arc. His face was calm but there was a gloating glint in his eyes. "That capsule is lodged right at the base of your father's brain stem, the exact same location as your mother's tumour. She had a cancerous time bomb ticking away inside her head. Now he has an actual bomb in his. It'll be a much quicker death than hers, of course, but no less permanent. Only you can prevent it from happening, Odysseus."

Od knew what was coming next.

"A trade," d'Arc said. "That's what I'm offering. Your father for the Warsuit. Surrender the Warsuit to me, and your father gets to live. I'm giving you sixty seconds to decide. Otherwise, I simply pluck the transmitter off my chest. The instant its sensor loses contact with my skin, the capsule detonates. There's enough PETN in there to entirely obliterate that magnificent brain of his."

He bared his wrist, on which hung a Rolex watch with a crocodile-hide strap.

"Your time starts... now."

CHAPTER 13

"Quick, Wes, what are our options?" said Od. "Shoot him?"

"But if we kill him, your father dies, and if we only wound him, he'll still be able to pull the transmitter off, or one of his men can do it for him."

"What if we shoot the transmitter itself? Destroy it?"

"Bad idea. It's keeping the bomb from going off. If it stops working, the detonator automatically discharges."

"Forty-five seconds left," d'Arc announced.

"Don't do it, Od," his father called out. "I'm not worth it. Don't let him have the suit at any cost. It's far too powerful to fall into the hands of a lunatic like d'Arc."

Od was growing frantic. "Can we maybe jam the

signal between the transmitter and the bomb?"

"Again, bad idea," said Wes. "Interfering with the transmission would set the bomb off. D'Arc's got us over a barrel, I'm afraid, Od. It's the suit or your father. There's nothing else."

"There must be!"

"Twenty-five seconds, Odysseus. Time's running out. I need an answer." D'Arc clasped the transmitter as if preparing to remove it from himself.

"Don't, Od!" his father called out. "I know what this man's plans for the world are. If he has the Warsuit, he'll be almost unstoppable. Millions will die. My life's nothing compared to that. Stay in there and blow the arrogant so-and-so to kingdom come."

"How noble!" d'Arc sneered. "Ten seconds, Odysseus. Nine. Eight..."

"Wes?" Od's throat was tight with fear.

"Your call. It's out of my hands. You decide what's best."

"Five. Four. Three."

"All right!" Od said over the external speaker. "All right. You win, d'Arc. It's yours. The suit is yours. On one condition. You take that bomb out of my dad's head, you hear me? Soon as I'm out, it's gone."

"Agreed," said d'Arc.

"Promise?"

"You have my word, and I am, trust me, a man who keeps his word."

Od didn't trust him. Once d'Arc had the Warsuit, however, what did he stand to gain from leaving the bomb inside Od's father?

"Then we have a deal," he said.

Tremaine Fitch dropped his head and let out a shuddering breath. Ready as he'd been to die, it was a relief not to have to.

"You've donc the right thing, Odysseus," said d'Arc.

"You're going to havc to give me a moment," Od said. "It's not easy getting in and out of this thing."

D'Arc bowed, generous in victory. "Take as long as you want." To Od's father he said, "I knew I'd be able to winkle the sardine out of the can. All it needed was the application of the right sort of pressure in the right spot."

"Oh, just shut up, will you?"

"Come now, don't be like that, professor. Nobody likes a sore loser. And contrary to your claims, I am not a lunatic. I have such dreams for the people of earth, such a glorious vision for the future!"

"You're a monster and a megalomaniac."

"Incorrect!" barked d'Arc. "But as I am the one who's holding your life in the balance, I'd advise you to keep a civil tongue in your head – or else you won't have a head at all. Ah! And here, if I'm not mistaken, is your youngster. The snail emerges from its shell."

The hatch in the Warsuit's back opened and Od wriggled out and jumped down. His limbs were numb and stiff from being confined in the suit for so many hours. He stretched them, joints cracking. Then he went over to his father.

"Dad? You all right?"

"All the better for seeing you, Od." Tremaine Fitch embraced his son, burying his face in Od's shoulder.

Od couldn't remember the last time his father had hugged him. Had he done it since his mother died? It felt good.

"You shouldn't have – " his father began.

"Don't," Od interrupted. "You know I had no choice."

"Family reunion," d'Arc crooned. "How touching."

"And you." Od rounded on him. "You pompous windbag. Time to keep your side of the bargain."

"Of course, of course," said d'Arc soothingly. He motioned to the end of the catwalk. "Our on-board doctor is right this way. He's waiting, in fact, all set to operate. You see, I knew you'd cave, Odysseus. It was a foregone conclusion. Love for a parent is one of the strongest motivations there is."

"How would you know? You killed yours."

D'Arc gave a slow, lizard-like blink. "I did not. That is a gross slander."

"Well, someone did."

"My parents are none of your business." D'Arc turned on his heel and set off along the catwalk. "Follow me, both of you Fitches," he said over his shoulder. "And you men." This was directed at the T-Cell operatives. "Get our best engineers down here. I want them pulling that Warsuit to bits pronto. I especially want that operating system out of it. That's the key to everything. Let's tear that software apart and find out what makes it tick."

Chapter 14

D'Arc led Od and his father through the submarine, along corridors and through wheel-lock doors and up and down companionway staircases. It was a vast, humming labyrinth, full of laboratories and workshops in which T-Cell personnel were busy constructing and testing and fine-tuning various pieces of equipment. Od got the sense of an industrious empire, a self-contained little world like an anthill, where countless drones were subservient to the ruling ant – d'Arc – and toiled all day long to do his bidding.

He also grasped that there were different classes of T-Celler and you could tell them apart by their uniforms. Combat operatives wore grey jumpsuits, while engineers wore blue and scientists green. This colour coding added to the whole anthill impression.

Everyone had a distinct role, like a soldier ant or a worker ant, knew their place, and could recognise their own kind at a glance.

"How was it?" Tremaine Fitch asked as they walked. "The suit? I have to know."

"Pretty cool," Od said.

"That's all?"

"No, all right, it was amazing."

"Thought so. Wes?"

"Worked like a charm. I got the feeling we were like friends, you know? He had my back, I had his. We sorted through problems together – though I was still the boss."

"Good, good. That was the general idea." In spite of their predicament, Od's father allowed himself a smile of self-congratulation. "The whole point was to make something that anyone could learn to use, without needing years of training. An incredibly sophisticated tool made super simple. And of course, people work better in partnerships than on their own. Humans are social animals. We need interaction. So why not extend that to our relationship with technology?"

"Yeah," said Od. "What's weird is, I miss Wes already. He's just zeroes and ones in a computer, when you get down to it. Just code. But he became... real, I guess."

"For the suit to feel like a part of you, an extension of yourself, there has to be feedback between you and it, a continuous dialogue. Just as there is between your conscious mind and your subconscious. Wes is designed to mimic the function of the human brain and nervous system in controlling the body. The more real he seems, the better the suit and the suit's wearer function together."

"All very remarkable," said d'Arc, "and your achievement, professor, will further T-Cell's cause no end. But we've arrived at the ship's sick bay. Here's where you can be rid of the burden of that bomb. In you go."

D'Arc held open the door with the red cross on it. The smell of antiseptic wafted out. Inside, a man in blue surgical scrubs was snapping on a pair of latex gloves. He beckoned to Professor Fitch, who went in. Od was about to follow but d'Arc held him back.

"Not you, young man. You and I, I think, should have a chat."

Od looked at his father.

"Go with him, son. I'm sure you'll be fine."

"What about you?"

"Well, this isn't going to be pleasant." Tremaine Fitch put on a brave face. "But you know what they say. Better out than in."

"Ten minutes, maybe less, and he'll be good as new," said d'Arc. "Let's put the time to profitable use. When you learn a bit more about what we're up to here aboard the *Lux Aurorae*, Odysseus, I predict you'll be inclined to judge us a little less harshly."

* * *

"They call us terrorists," said d'Arc, "but then that's the crude label that has been stuck on freedom fighters down through the centuries. Anyone who challenges the establishment, threatens the status quo, gets demonised like that. Even Jesus was considered a dangerous radical. That's why the Romans got rid of him."

Od and d'Arc were standing on the bridge of the *Lux Aurorae*, a control room where a crew of twenty sat at consoles and collaboratively navigated the immense vessel through the waters. Their T-Cell uniforms were white. Dominating the space was a monitor as big as a cinema screen, which relayed the view from a camera mounted on the submarine's prow. Plankton and specks of floating organic debris glittered against an indigo backdrop, swirling like a heavy snowfall. Now and then a fish finned into view and darted away just as swiftly. A shoal of squid jetted past in V-formation, their skin aglow with ripples of bioluminescence.

"The fact is," d'Arc went on, "we in T-Cell stand in opposition to a great injustice. We aim to correct an imbalance that is in danger of tearing the world apart. I'm talking about the technology gap – the gulf between the haves and have-nots, between the countries which want for nothing when it comes to modern conveniences and the ones which are condemned to an almost medieval level of existence by their lack of access to even the most basic consumer goods."

"You mean the developed world and the developing world."

"More or less. In industrialised nations we go through technology like we go through a box of tissues – use and discard, use and discard. People change their computers yearly, mobile phones monthly, with scarcely a thought. Never mind the environmental cost of such wastefulness. What about those who have nothing? The poor nations where a phone costs a year's salary and a laptop is an unimaginable luxury? Why should they go without when others enjoy such abundance?"

"But that's all changing," said Od.

"Is it?"

"Yeah. Our class did a hook-up at school with a school in Botswana. We communicated with them for a term using email and Skype. It was quite good fun, actually."

"One school in Botswana. A single school, in one of the few stable and prosperous African nations. But still, overall, the rate of inequality increases. The technology gap continues to grow. And then there are the inventions that could improve the lives of everyone, rich and poor alike, and yet are sidelined or ignored by governments, and sometimes even deliberately kept under wraps."

"Like the everlasting lightbulb? The car that runs on water? Those old rumours?"

"You may scoff, but as with all conspiracy theories there's a grain of truth there," said d'Arc. "Big corporations – the oil companies, the utility companies – do all they can to suppress revolutionary new sources of energy or power-saving devices.

Anything that could damage their monopolies or their profits, they ruthlessly crush and quash. Governments go along with it because they're in the corporations' pockets. It's a worldwide scandal – top-down cronyism that's fleecing the public. Not to mention ruining the planet and inflicting misery on millions thanks to climate change."

"So you're eco-warriors, is that it?"

"Warriors, yes. Eco? Not so much. Progress is our aim – free and fair progress for all."

Od noticed for the first time that one of d'Arc's eyes was slightly discoloured. Within his left iris there was a bright red spot about the size of the head of a nail. It stood out against the iris's pale brown like a drop of blood on a copper penny.

"But you kill to get your way," he said.

"We must," sighed d'Arc. "The only way to effect any kind of meaningful change in the global situation is violence. Governments protect their own interests with weapons and soldiers. We must meet their militarism with militarism of our own. I dearly wish it were otherwise."

"And that's where the Warsuit comes in. You want to copy it. You want to mass-produce thousands of your own, make a huge army of Warsuits."

"Too costly," said d'Arc, with a shake of his head. "Too time-consuming. What we want is simply your father's control software."

"Wes."

"That's the acronym you know it by, yes. We want to install a Wes in all of our fighter aircraft to make them more agile, more responsive to commands, more intuitive to their pilots' needs and wishes. Not to mention make it possible for our personnel, many of whom have no professional combat experience, to fly them. It'll give us the edge over the military might of every nation when – " He stopped himself.

"When what?" Od prompted. "Come on, you were about to spill the beans on the Big Plan. You can tell me. What am I going to do about it? I'm just a kid. How *are* T-Cell going to bring about this new, better, fairer world of yours? I'm all ears. Dying to know. Bet it involves murdering a whole bunch of people."

"Your insolence borders on insult, Odysseus Fitch," d'Arc snapped. "Do not provoke me. It would be fatally foolish if you did. However..." He relaxed a little. His oily smoothness returned. "I don't see the harm in outlining the basics to you. You and your father won't be leaving this sub any time soon. Yes, conflict is a part of it. The old ways need to be cast aside – forcibly. The existing order must be overthrown. Governments must be toppled, the apparatus of state dismantled. A fresh start must be made, and conflict is the means to that end. The only possible means."

"Destroy civilisation and – "

"And rebuild it."

"In the way *you* decide it needs to be rebuilt."

"The right way. With an equal share of everything among everyone. No more instability. A bright, technology-enriched future for all."

"With you in charge, lording it over everyone else."

"Someone has to be the figurehead and inspiration. It might as well be someone as deserving and qualified as me."

"Never mind that it'll take a bloodbath to achieve this magic happyland future of yours."

"In olden times, in some societies, it was believed that bathing in blood was a cleansing process," said d'Arc. "It could cure diseases."

"Nice."

Before d'Arc could respond, the trigger transmitter on his chest let out a beep. "Ah," he said, inspecting it. The diode had gone out. "That means the capsule is out of your father. All's well." He plucked the trigger off and tossed it aside. Then he frowned at Od.

"What were you just doing?"

"Nothing," said Od. He quickly raised his hand from where it had been, loitering beside his jeans pocket.

"You're looking shifty."

"I, er..." Od fumbled for an excuse. "I just caught sight of your eye. I – I didn't want to stare, that's all. In case you're, you know, self-conscious about it."

"My eye? You're referring to my red spot. Yes, unusual, isn't it? Interestingly, that's how I came by my given name. My father noticed the spot when I was born and it reminded him of the famous Great Red Spot on the face of the planet Jupiter. He was something of an astronomy buff, my old man. I hated it when I was little. I got teased about it. Now, rather than a disfigurement, I regard it as a unique distinguishing feature."

The T-Cell leader mused for a moment, glancing at the image of himself reflected on the shiny surface of a console. He seemed to like what he saw there.

"Where was I?" he said. "Oh yes. Bloodbaths. I would much prefer to keep civilian casualties to a minimum. But strength and superior firepower are essential to success. Here on the *Lux Aurorae*, and at a number of other secret locations, I have amassed fleets of extraordinary combat vehicles. They have been designed by brilliant minds from across the planet, men and women who share my goals and vision. We stand, together, on the brink of bringing our dream to fruition. The Warsuit interface will provide the finishing touch, the last element we need to make our forces invincible. Would that your father had been willing to share his genius freely. It became clear as soon as we had him in our possession that he wasn't going to play along. Hence we had to resort to drastic measures, ultimately involving you. I sincerely regret that. Children should not have to suffer for their parents' mistakes."

"The only mistake my dad made, as I see it, was starting in on the Warsuit project in the first place."

"Ah well, he didn't have much of a choice there."

Od frowned. "No choice? You're saying he was blackmailed into it?"

"Not blackmailed. No, I'm afraid *I'm* responsible, in a roundabout way, for your father's decision to throw in his lot with the British government. You see, Odysseus, it was as a direct consequence of T-Cell activity that Professor Fitch switched professions, abandoning the academic life to become a weaponsmith. An act of technological liberation went awry, alas, and the result was – ”

“Sir?”

“Yes?” D’Arc turned. Addressing him was a grizzled woman in her sixties who had hair the colour of a battleship. “What is it, Captain Marquez?”

“Sorry to interrupt, but there’s a message for you from the hangar. Chief Engineer Fortgang would like a word. Urgently.”

“Put him on speakerphone.”

“Λye aye.” Captain Marqucz rclaycd thc order to the communications officer.

“Mr Fortgang,” said d’Arc, pressing a button on a microphone. “How may I help?”

“Sir,” said the chief engineer’s disembodied voice, “we... er... we appear to have a slight problem.”

“What sort of problem?”

“The Warsuit. It – it’s started to behave erratically.”

D’Arc’s eyes narrowed and his mouth tightened at the corners. “Erratically how? Elucidate, Fortgang. Be precise.”

“It’s... Well, I suppose you could say it’s not co-operating. You really need to come and see for yourself, Mr d’Arc.”

"Very well. I shall." D'Arc switched the mike off and spun round to glare at Od. "Is this your doing? It is, isn't it?"

"Not me," Od said, all innocence.

"Don't lie, boy. Don't even try." D'Arc was doing everything he could to keep his cool. He wasn't succeeding. "What have you done? Have you sabotaged the suit in some way? You'd better not have, both for your sake and your father's."

"Honest, I haven't sabotaged anything."

"Come with me." D'Arc signalled curtly to the two T-Cellers who had accompanied him and Od to the bridge. They grabbed Od by the scruff of the neck and frogmarched him out, following in their leader's wake.

Od knew that the next few minutes were crucial. If he didn't get everything right, it would be curtains for him and his dad. And the outlook for the rest of humankind wouldn't be any too rosy either.

CHAPTER 15

A handful of T-Cell engineers were gathered on the hangar catwalk. They were keeping their distance from Warsuit 1.0, and with good reason. The suit was spinning the barrels on its right arm, stopping every so often to select one, then spinning them again. Flaps opened and shut, revealing the bombs and defensive devices that were stashed all over its body.

The T-Cellers muttered amongst themselves in consternation. They feared the seven-metre-tall machine was going to go on the attack at any moment.

"What's all this?" d'Arc boomed as he arrived on the scene with Od in tow. "Why are you all cowering like that? Fortgang! An explanation, if you please."

"Sir," said the Chief Engineer nervously. "As you can see, the suit seems to be in threat assessment mode. It just started a few minutes ago. Nobody had even touched it yet. I think it's trying to choose a weapon. Which is bizarre. From what I understand, it can't be active because there's nobody inside. It should still be dormant."

"Precisely! Use your head, man. The suit can't function without a pilot."

"Some kind of software glitch, then," Fortgang hazarded. "A bug in the system."

"Or – " d'Arc glared at Od " – deceit. How did you manage it, boy?"

"I'm sorry, I – "

Od didn't get to finish the sentence. D'Arc slapped him across the cheek, not hard but sharply enough to sting.

"Next time it'll be a punch. Answer me. None of your tomfoolery, now."

Od was going to ask what tomfoolery was, as he'd never heard the word before, but he thought better of it. Instead he said, "OK, it's a fair cop." He drew his phone out of his pocket. "I'm sending Wes a voice message I recorded beforehand, on constant repeat. It's telling him to select barrels and initiate then cancel weapons. I set it all up just before I climbed out, and I hit Send when we were on the bridge, once I knew the bomb was safely out of my dad."

"Oh, very ingenious." D'Arc snatched the phone out of Od's hand. "But I don't see the point. All I have to do is press Disconnect and the suit goes inert again. What on earth could you hope to gain from your little prank?"

Od shrugged. "Seemed like a good idea at the time."

"But not good enough." D'Arc poised his thumb over the phone. "Let's put an end to this nonsense."

"I wouldn't do that if I were you," Od warned.

D'Arc glanced at him, sneered, and brought his thumb down on the cut-off button.

Warsuit 1.0 immcdiatcly fell still.

"There," d'Arc said. "You know, you've gone down in my estimation, lad. All you've done here is waste time. You seem quite bright, and yet this is so... *petty*. I hope you're pleased with yourself, because no one else is."

"Oh, I am," said Od. "Because I also instructed Wes to do something as soon as the messages stop coming."

D'Arc looked towards the Warsuit, then back at Od. His lips pursed, betraying just the tiniest hint of concern. "Instructed it to do what?"

"You put the idea in my head with that trigger thing of yours. No more signal equals detonation. Same principle here, only with a different kind of result."

"What have you done? Ordered the suit to self-destruct?"

"Wouldn't know how."

D'Arc seized Od by the shoulders and shook him. "Then *what*?" he bellowed. Flecks of spittle hit Od's face.

"That," Od said quietly, pointing.

From an aperture in Warsuit 1.0's chest, two nozzles protruded. Twin streams of liquid began to jet out, one of them clear, the other chalky white. Where the liquids met and mingled on the catwalk floor, the metal began to sizzle and steam.

"Carborane superacid," said Od. "A million times more corrosive than sulphuric acid. Wes told me it can eat through anything. I'd say we have about fifteen seconds before this catwalk splits in two and we all slide off. And it's a pretty long drop, isn't it?"

Already holes were appearing in the centimetre-thick steel floor. The acrid stench of acid vapour filled the air. The T-Cell engineers started to back away, murmuring anxiously. Several turned and took to their heels. The two inert substances that combined to form the acid, solvent and catalyst, continued to spout from the Warsuit.

"I can't believe you'd do such a thing," d'Arc hissed. "You wretched little – "

Od twisted out of his grasp and broke into a run. The engineers were making for the far end, where the catwalk was attached to the gallery that ran round the rim of the hangar. They would be safe there. Od, however, went in the opposite direction, towards the centre of the catwalk, where the Warsuit stood.

"Get him!" d'Arc yelled. "Shoot the brat!"

But the two T-Cell paramilitaries were retreating also. The catwalk was letting out groans and squeals and shuddering violently. It was losing structural integrity and felt ready to give way at any moment.

Od leapt over the puddle of acid and the widening, ragged gap it was creating. Globs of melted metal dropped off the edge of it as he landed heavily on the other side. Without pause, he clambered up the back of the Warsuit, finding handholds and toeholds in its vents and knee joints, and swung himself inside.

"Wes!"

The catwalk let out a grinding shriek and broke partly in half, sagging over at an angle. Warsuit 1.0 lurched sideways but stayed upright, just.

"Od, nice to have you back," said Wes. "The ruse worked, I see."

"Yeah, yeah, no time for back-patting," said Od. "The catwalk's about to go. We need to go too."

"Firing thrusters in three, two – "

The catwalk couldn't stay up any longer. The acid had dissolved it all the way across. It snapped in half, and neither end could support its own weight. Both halves broke free from their moorings and fell. They plunged, tumbling end over end, into the pit of the hangar, where they landed with a tremendous, ringing double *clang* that sounded like a pair of gigantic gongs being struck.

Warsuit 1.0, however, did not fall with them. It hovered on its thrusters, which had ignited the very same instant the catwalk collapsed.

"Yes!" hissed Od.

He'd half hoped that Jupiter d'Arc would be still on the catwalk when it collapsed, but no such luck. D'Arc's sense of self-preservation had kicked in and he had scrambled to safety like all the other T-Cellers. He was with them now on the gallery, and he looked, to say the least, pretty cheesed off.

"What now, Od?" Wes enquired.

"Now, my friend," Od said, "we bring a little Warsuit-style mayhem!"

CHAPTER 16

The magnetised nano-thermite charge clunked into place on the underside of the hangar hatch. Wes had done the calculations. The hatch doors were half a metre thick. The nano-thermite, powerful as it was, could not blow a hole clean through. But if positioned just right, at the seam where they joined, it would cause enough damage to spring a leak.

And a leak on a submarine was the worst thing that could happen, an undersea sailor's nightmare.

Warsuit 1.0 flew back from the hatch, retreating to a safe distance.

"Let's hope we've worked this out right," Od said.

"I'm confident," said Wes.

Wish I was, Od thought.

"Detonate charge?"

"Go on. Do it."

The charge went off, a burst of blinding yellow followed by billowing clouds of thick black smoke.

As the smoke cleared, Od studied the result.

Nothing. Just a white star-shaped scar on the doors. The metal was distorted but hardly so as you'd notice.

"Oh well. So much for that." Od was vaguely relieved. The plan he and Wes had concocted was an extremely high-risk strategy. It was as likely to cause catastrophe as save the day.

Then a trickle of water appeared, dribbling down. It spread, strengthened, and rapidly became a gushing spurt.

Instantly, alarms blared throughout the *Lux Aurorae*. Emergency lights whirled and a loud recorded voice intoned, "Hull breach. All personnel to life pods. Hull breach. All personnel to life pods. This is not a drill. Repeat, this is not a drill."

* * *

On the bridge a grim-faced Captain Marquez did what she had to. "Blow ballast in the saddle tanks," she ordered. "Forward all engines, flank speed. Hydroplanes to vertical fore and aft. Rise! Rise! Rise!"

The *Lux Aurorae* charged upwards from the depths, propellers churning. The great submarine was canted at a shallow angle and making 20 knots, an incredible speed for a craft so huge. Her hull groaned. Bulkheads strained. Rivets popped. Throughout her length it was panic stations as people sprinted to the evacuation assembly points. They collided with one another, sometimes trampling over one another in their desperation. The busy efficiency of moments ago had given way to total frenzy. These were no longer T-Cellers. They were ordinary, terrified men and women who didn't care about their shared cause any more, only about getting out of the sub alive. Their overriding impulse wasn't creating a better world, it was avoiding being drowned.

Only one among them was focused on something other than saving himself. That was Jupiter d'Arc. While everyone else crammed into the life pods and braced themselves for being jettisoned into the water, d'Arc shinned down a ladder and ran to one of the Hexaflyers. He climbed in through the hold, hurried past the benches that could hold up to twenty operatives, and shinned up a ladder to the cockpit.

Normally a Hexaflyer carried a three-strong crew – pilot, co-pilot and navigator – but the extra pilot was simply a precaution in case the main pilot suddenly fell ill mid-journey and the navigator was a luxury to free up the other two so they could concentrate on flying. The aircraft could be flown solo, and that was what d'Arc intended to do.

He slipped on the radio headset and hit the ignition switches. The vanes in the six propulsion units began to turn. He grasped the joystick and eased the throttle handle towards him to increase power. The gunship rose, folded its undercarriage and glided slowly forwards. Through the cockpit canopy d'Arc spied Warsuit 1.0, hovering aloft as water continued to pour in through the damaged hatch. He bared his teeth and started throwing switches, arming every weapon the Hexaflyer carried.

Odysseus Fitch, d'Arc thought. *You think you're so smart. You think you've thwarted my plans. We'll just see about that.*

* * *

"Od..."

"Spotted it, Wes. That Hexaflyer that's lifting off. Zoom in on the pilot."

"Jupiter d'Arc."

"Yeah, thought as much. Doesn't look too amused, does he?"

"Not in the slightest," said Wes.

D'Arc's voice over the radio confirmed it. "I know you can hear me, Odysseus, so listen, and listen well. You do not do this, not to me, Jupiter d'Arc. You do not endanger the lives of my people and imperil my ship and think you won't somehow have to pay the price. The *Lux Aurorae* is going to have to surface now, and the moment she does, she'll show up on every spy satellite in the region. Something her size will be impossible to miss. She'll be hidden from prying eyes no longer, every government in the world will know where she is, and her usefulness will therefore be at an end. No doubt that was your intention. But in doing so, you've seriously interfered with everything I've been working towards, and for that you must die."

"Hey, you started it, not me," Od answered. "You've only got yourself to blame. If you hadn't kidnapped my dad, none of this would have happened."

"I hope you've enjoyed your life, short as it's been," d'Arc snarled. "It's just about to come to a premature end."

"Bring it on, spotty eye," Od said with as much bravado as he could muster.

"Oh, I most certainly shall."

The Hexaflyer nosed its way out into the open.

"All his onboard weapons systems are primed," said Wes. "He means business."

Next thing Od knew, two missiles had detached themselves from the gunship's underside and were winging their way towards Warsuit 1.0.

"Heat-seekers," said Wes. "They're homing in on our thrusters."

"Countermeasures!" said Od.

"No time."

"Then cut the thrusters."

"We'll fall."

"Do it anyway!"

The boot thrusters were extinguished and Warsuit 1.0 dropped like a rock. The missiles, having lost the dual heat signatures they were tracking, shot dumbly onwards. They passed over the top of the plummeting Warsuit and impacted among the aircraft on the other side of the hangar. Huge fiery flowers blossomed.

The *Lux Aurorae* was rocked by the force of the explosions inside her but continued her upward progress. Above, on the surface of the Atlantic, a dome of water was forming. The pressure wave generated by the rising submarine built up a kind of liquid blister that grew to several metres in height. As it swelled, it spat out the fish inside it like tiny silver sparks.

Meanwhile, Warsuit 1.0 reignited its thrusters within inches of striking the waterlogged hangar floor. The sudden reversal of direction jarred Od's spine. It felt as though all his vertebrae were being squashed together. A wave of light-headedness washed through him, but there was little time to recover. Wes was already alerting him to another missile coming from the Hexaflyer, this one laser-targeted rather than heat-seeking.

"It's hardened. Can't get in. He's launched it."

"Then evasive action."

The missile chased Warsuit 1.0 through the hangar space. Wes jinked and rolled and zigzagged, all at top speed, but the missile kept up. The gap between the two, missile and suit, closed remorselessly, metre by metre. Od was both terrified and nauseated. The Warsuit's dragonfly aerobatics would have made even an experienced fighter ace airsick.

"Can't... take... much more... of this," he gasped. His head swam. He felt close to blacking out.

"Understood," Wes agreed. "One chance. A last-ditch, crazy manoeuvre. If I get it wrong, it'll mean the end of us as surely as that missile will. Do you trust me?"

If Wes had posed this question in anyone's voice other than Tremaine Fitch's, Od would have said no.

"Yes."

"Then hang on. This is going to be tight."

Warsuit 1.0 made a sharp turn and soared towards the hatch and its fountaining downpour of seawater. The missile duly swung about and pursued. Od watched the hatch get closer and realised what Wes was attempting. His whole body went rigid.

"Turn, Wes."

"Not yet."

"Turn!"

"One second more."

"*Turn!*"

"Now!" cried Wes.

Warsuit 1.0 abruptly changed course, veering through ninety degrees, just missing the hatch. The missile couldn't match the suit's agility in the air. It rammed nose-first into the hatch and its warhead went off with a bang that made a thunderclap sound tame. Both the doors erupted outwards. The Warsuit was sent spiralling through the air.

At that exact moment, the large blister in the ocean's surface popped. The *Lux Aurorae* breached like a whale coming up for air, and the mound of water shattered into white surf.

Had the hatch exploded any earlier than it did, thousands of tons of seawater would have come sluicing into the hangar and the *Lux Aurorae* would have been swamped and sunk like a stone. Wes had not simply been fortunate in his timing, however. Luck had had nothing to do with it. He had been aware of the submarine's position in the water and known she was just about to emerge into the air.

Or so he told Od, who had no choice but to believe him.

"Cut it fine, though, didn't you?" Od said, still reeling from the concussion of the missile blast. The hatch doors were now like two steel petals, opened to the sky.

"The margin of error was narrow but acceptable," Wes replied. "I'd never be entirely reckless when lives are at stake. Especially yours, Od. Speaking of which... Hexaflyer at six o'clock."

As the T-Cell aircraft rose from below, its pilot's voice came snarking over the airwaves. "Missed you twice, Odysseus, but you know what they say – third time's the charm."

"Face it, d'Arc," Od said, "you've lost. Once I'm sure everyone's got off this submarine safely, including my dad, I'm going to lob a few big bombs at it and send it to join the *Titanic* on the ocean floor."

"You'll never get the chance. Did I mention, by the way, that I'm to blame for your father building that suit?"

"You did. You never got round to saying how, though, and frankly, I'm not sure I care."

"You will care when I tell you. Your mother, remember her?"

"What about my mother?" said Od tautly.

"Her operation going awry – the cause wasn't human error, as you were told. Actually it was us, T-Cell."

"Go on." Od felt his stomach clench. Something uncoiled in his heart like a venomous snake stirring from sleep.

"I instigated a cyber attack on the Oncodyne Clinic that day," d'Arc said. "We were after the secrets of the ion beam and hoped to pluck them out of the clinic's mainframe while the beam was in use. The attack coincided with your mother's time in the operating theatre, and it upset the minute calibration of the laser. Alas, what was meant to kill the tumour ended up scything through her brain. The ion beam became like a mad axeman running amok, doing irreparable harm. The surgeons fought to reset the machine and save her, but the damage was too extensive. The poor woman died right there and then on the operating table."

"This is crap. I don't believe a word of it."

"You do, though. How would I know all these details if it wasn't true?"

"Shut up. Just shut your mouth."

"How does that make you feel, Odysseus? Knowing that T-Cell took your mother from you? It's obvious how it made your father feel. It twisted him up inside. It turned him from a humble, harmless academic into a builder of death machines. Oh, he was well aware of the true circumstances of his wife's demise. The British government made sure of that. They used it to recruit him. Once they'd told him how his wife really died, they didn't have to do much arm-twisting, though. Jumped at the chance, he did."

"Od," said Wes, "he's trying to rile you."

"He's succeeding."

"But the whole point is to stop you thinking clearly. He wants you upset and confused so you'll do something irrational and stupid."

"Then," said Od, "he can't know me very well, can he? I'm riled all right. But I've never been clearer-headed in my life. Let's get out of here, Wes. It's too cramped inside this sub. We need elbow room."

Warsuit 1.0 exited up through the torn hatch. As it rose above the *Lux Aurorae*, Od saw slots open all along the submarine's length, just below the waterline. Next moment, spheres popped out like peas from the shell. They surged to the surface, righting themselves and floating. They were the sub's life pods, and in each was a score of T-Cellers. One of them, Od was certain, contained his father. It wouldn't take long to find out which. The top section of each pod was fitted with panes of clear plexiglass. Wes could remote-scan the faces of the people inside until he spotted Tremaine Fitch.

The Hexaflyer shimmied up through the hatch. Od got ready for d'Arc to resume the fight, but instead the T-Cell leader turned his sights on the life pods. The Hexaflyer began strafing them with gunfire.

"What the...? You're shooting at your own people!" Od yelled at d'Arc.

"Plenty more where they came from," d'Arc replied. "It's your father I'm hoping to get. Sooner or later I'll find the one he's in."

A pod took a direct hit and erupted in flames. Its occupants leapt out frantically into the sea and started swimming away as the pod, a broken eggshell, began to sink.

"That does it," said Od. "Wes?"

"Say no more."

Warsuit 1.0 swooped on the Hexaflyer, hammering it with bullets. D'Arc had no choice but to leave the life pods alone and engage with Od. The Warsuit came out of its dive and started to climb, drawing the Hexaflyer after it, away from the life pods. D'Arc unleashed a volley of missiles. At Od's command Wes deployed countermeasures. Chaff bombs burst. The dazzling clouds of tinfoil flakes threw the missiles off-course and made them detonate prematurely. Heavy-calibre machinegun fire raked through the air at the Warsuit. Wes dodged, dived and darted around the blazing streams of bullets. Od retaliated with a blockbuster, but the Hexaflyer's own countermeasures bamboozled the shell and it crashed uselessly into the sea.

Hexaflyer and Warsuit battled it out in the sky

above the *Lux Aurorae* for several minutes. They seemed, to the people observing from the life pods, to be evenly matched. Neither could gain an edge on the other. Jupiter d'Arc had some skill as a pilot and the Hexaflyer was the faster of the two aircraft, but the Warsuit was extraordinarily deft and manoeuvrable. Explosions cracked and rumbled. As dogfights went, it was as dramatic and startling as any the audience below had seen.

For Od, there was little fear. There was no space for it in him. He was filled to the brim with a cool, calculating hatred. D'Arc had killed his mother. Had ruined his life, and his father's. Had tried to kill his father.

Payback. Justice. That was all Od wanted.

"We're starting to run low," Wes warned.

"On what?"

"Everything. Ordnance. Solid fuel. We've not much more than a minute's flying time left, and we're down to our last clip of bullets."

"So what does that leave?"

"The microwave beam, but that's only good for melting holes in things at close range. Apart from that, we've used up the lot."

Od glanced at the Hexaflyer in the rear view

screen. It was circling round, gaining altitude so that d'Arc could commence a fresh onslaught. Unlike Od, d'Arc hadn't yet thrown everything he had at his opponent. There was still plenty of the gunship's deadly payload left beneath its wings.

"How close is close range?"

"A couple of metres. Od, you're not seriously thinking..."

"I'm *very* seriously thinking. We're out of fuel. Out of ammo. Basically out of other options. If we go back down and land on that sub, we'll be a sitting duck."

"Correction. *I* would be a sitting duck. You could climb out and take cover."

"No. Anyway, if we don't stop d'Arc, he'll just start blasting away at the life pods again. He's not going to give up until I'm dead. And the feeling's kind of mutual. We do this, Wes. We finish him. We have to."

"If you say so," said Wes, and Od could hear the unspoken implication: *It's your funeral.*

The Hexaflyer had completed its turn and was making its approach run. D'Arc was coming out of the sun, whose rays made the aircraft's silver skin blaze as blindingly as a magnesium flare.

Warsuit 1.0 levelled out and went to meet it head on, boot thrusters burning bright blue. The two flying machines narrowed in on each other. Od could see a magnified image of d'Arc in the cockpit, his teeth clamped in a death's head grin. No words needed to be said. It was a midair game of chicken. Which of them would blink? Which would veer away at the last possible instant?

The answer was Warsuit 1.0. But only slightly. Wes flipped up over the Hexaflyer, then swooped in behind, riding its slipstream. A snap of acceleration, a few adjustments in pitch and attitude, and the Warsuit landed on the Hexaflyer's back, straddling its fuselage.

Immediately Od lowered the suit's left arm. The pincer-dish arrangement at the end began to glow orange-hot, red-hot, white-hot. The surface of the Hexaflyer's portside wing began to glow in the same colours. Aluminium rippled and bubbled and began trickling back towards the ailerons like streams of mercury.

D'Arc grasped what was being done to his aircraft and threw the gunship into a series of spins, rolls and turns. Wes compensated as best he could with the thrusters in order to keep the suit steady and maintain position. Od concentrated on training the microwave beam on a single spot, or trying to. The wing was melting, but not as fast or as evenly as he would have liked. To sever it all the way through was going to take time and a lack of interference. D'Arc was giving neither.

Finally one of d'Arc's sudden sharp turns managed to dislodge Warsuit 1.0's footing. The Warsuit slithered across the wing on its side, fetching up against one of the propulsion units. Seeing this, d'Arc thrust the joystick forwards and put the Hexaflyer into a near-vertical dive. Od managed to hook the suit's right arm around the propulsion unit and hang on, just. D'Arc barrel-rolled. Still Od clung on grimly, although the centripetal force nearly hurled the Warsuit off.

"The propulsion unit," said Wes. "It's our only chance. The next move d'Arc makes will toss us clear, and that'll be that."

"Surely if we blow it up at point-blank range – "

"We get blown up too."

"Can the suit take it?"

Wes was silent for a beat, then said, "Does it matter?"

And Od understood that it didn't matter. Not

compared with stopping d'Arc. Ending T-Cell's terrorism by cutting off its head.

He brought his left arm up and directed the microwave beam into the mouth of the propulsion unit.

There was fire.

And noise.

And a sickening carousel of turning, wheeling, somersaulting, up-ending, spinning.

And the screech of tortured metal.

And the dim roar of thrusters.

And then a bone-shaking impact.

Followed by another.

And another.

All the screens went black. The lights went out.

Od couldn't tell if he was in darkness or unconscious.

Was there any difference?

CHAPTER 17

A cabin on a naval vessel. A hard, narrow bunk bed. The slow, ponderous up and down of a large ship stationary at sea.

Od crawled out from under the covers and got blearily to his feet. His head throbbed. His body was a mass of bruises. He needed to pee badly.

As he stumbled towards the door in search of a toilet, he bumped into two people entering the cabin.

That was when he realised he was wearing just his underpants.

One of the people was his father, so the near-nudity didn't matter so much. The other, however, was Angelica W-K. The brief, appraising look she cast over Od's body made him whirl round and snatch a blanket off the bunk to cover himself with.

"I've seen worse," she sniffed. "Seen better, too."

* * *

An hour later, Od was dressed, fed, dosed up on painkillers and out on the main deck of the HMS *Dominator*. In the light of a spectacular sunset the Royal Navy destroyer lay at anchor beside the *Lux Aurorae*. It was a large ship, 150 metres from stem to stern, but dwarfed by the island-like bulk of the crippled submarine. A second Royal Navy vessel, a frigate called the *Imperial*, was nearby. Both ships had been on exercises near Madeira when the call came in from Angelica W-K redirecting them to this location. She herself had been flown out by Sea King helicopter and been winched aboard the *Dominator* en route.

"We were tracking you," she had told Od earlier in the cabin, after he had filled her in on everything he had done since their last conversation. "The Warsuit's fitted with a GPS transponder, naturally. We lost the signal when you went under the waves. We assumed that you'd crashed and this would be a retrieval operation."

"Pulling my body up from the water in my seven-metre metal coffin, you mean."

"Indeed. Little did we realise it would be a mopping-up operation instead."

She didn't smile. Od didn't think she was capable of it. But her blood-red mouth did go a fraction less rigid.

"Two hundred T-Cell operatives are now in our custody," she went on, "and we've secured one of their main bases. This sub has been eluding everyone for years. We knew she existed but could never find her. Now and then various navies have picked up mysterious sonar traces which had to be her. You'd think something so big would be hard to miss, but her sheer size has been her greatest disguise. The sonar pings that come back from her register her as a rock formation, an undersea ridge that shouldn't be there, and she's moved on before anyone can get a better fix on her."

"Well, she's all yours now."

"Yes." Angelica W-K looked like she was about to say thank you, but it seemed that gratitude, like smiling, was beyond her.

"And d'Arc?" Od almost didn't want to ask the question. He assumed the T-Cell leader must be dead, which made him a murderer. Never mind that he had been provoked. Never mind that the world was a far better place without d'Arc in it. Guilt was guilt. Od's conscience would have a heavy burden to bear for years to come, maybe forever.

"Actually, we're not sure." Angelica W-K turned to Od's father. "You say his aircraft hit the sea."

"It did," said Tremaine Fitch. "It went down in flames, minus a wing but more or less in one piece. I saw it bounce along like a skimming stone, then sink. It's just conceivable he could have survived, perhaps even bailed out before he went down. But I doubt it. Let's hope not."

"Well, by all accounts, it was either you or him, Od," said Angelica W-K. "Be glad it was you."

Od tried to draw comfort from her words. It wasn't easy.

"The Warsuit," he said. "What's happened to it?"

Now he was out on deck and able to see for himself the state Warsuit 1.0 was in.

The suit lay on top of the *Lux Aurorae* in several pieces. A leg was smashed up. An arm had broken off and come to rest several metres away. The torso was battered and scraped. The head had a huge dent in it. The Warsuit was hardly recognisable as the gleaming, sleek machine it had once been.

"Wes saved you," Tremaine Fitch said. He was

standing beside Od at the handrail on the *Dominator*'s starboard side. "After you blew up d'Arc's aircraft, Wes used the thrusters to try and break your fall. All the way down he was doing his utmost to get you onto the deck of the submarine and give you as soft a landing as possible."

"Will he be OK?" The *Imperial* was extending a crane arm out over the submarine in order to haul the Warsuit parts aboard.

"If the CPU's intact, he will. The vital hardware components are ruggedized, but the suit still took a lot of damage. I'll only know once I've got all the bits back at the lab at Selston and can run tests. But I won't be starting work on that for a while."

"Why not?"

"Because I'd rather spend a bit of quality time with you. When was the last time we did anything together, you and me?"

"Just today, when we took down a terrorist organisation."

"Apart from that, smartass. Besides, you did most of the work. I've not been much of a dad to you lately, Od, and that has to change. There's lots we have to talk about. Your mum, for starters."

"But not now," said Od. "Some other time."

Od's father looked at him. "You're right. Another time. Let's just savour this." He put an arm around Od's shoulders. "You did well, you know. Fantastically well. You should be proud of yourself. I know I am. Mind you," he added, as a thought struck him, "seeing what you've done to my Warsuit, I'm wondering if I should ever let you learn to drive. I mean, if *that* is the way you treat an expensive vehicle, maybe you shouldn't be allowed near a car. At least not till you're much older."

"Dad, your Land Rover is not expensive."

"It has sentimental value. I'm very fond of that old banger, and I don't think I like the idea of you being behind the wheel." He chuckled. "Only kidding."

Od chuckled too. Then suddenly he remembered.

"Ah. Yeah. That's a point. Dad?"

Professor Fitch frowned. "What?"

"About the car..."